D0886269

STAY INFORMED

I'd love to stay in touch! You can email me at kathleen@ kathleentroy.com

For updates about new releases, as well as exclusive promotions, visit my website and sign up for the VIP mailing list. Head there now to receive a free story

www.kathleentroy.com

Enjoying the series? Help others discover *Dylan's Dilemma* by sharing with a friend.

ALSO BY KATHLEEN TROY

Dylan's Dog Squad Series

Dylan's Dilemma

Dylan's Dream

Dylan's Villain

Never Believe Series

Never Believe in Luck Twice

(Prologue/short story to Never Believe a Lie Twice)

Never Believe a Lie Twice

Coming soon: Never Believe a Con Artist Twice

DYLAN'S DREAM

KATHLEEN TROY

DYLAN AND FRIENDS PUBLISHING COMPANY

To Dylan,
My Little Buddy.

Your dreams should scare you...
and make you want to try harder.
-Dylan

ONE

"Where's your mom?"

"Hi, to you, too." Casey moved aside to let in Roger, the owner of Dream Big K-9 Academy.

A white cloth bandage, the size of a small life preserver, was wrapped around Roger's head. His second and third fingers were taped to a splint. His right eye was swollen and looked like a purple-and-black pansy.

Dylan sniffed at the fresh batch of cuts, bruises, and bandages on Roger's hairy legs. *Dogs don't like you.*

Casey smirked. "What happened? Get beat up by a Rottweiler?"

Roger rolled his shoulders back. "It's a jungle out there, kid."

"If dog training is so tough, why do you do it?"

"Three ex-wives and a bunch of no neck monster kids." Roger pointed his iPad at him. "Know what the secret of life is? Don't grow up. Get yourself a hut on some tax-free island like Barbados." He brought his face close to Casey's. "Remember that."

Dylan looked up at Casey. *What's an island?*

"Oh, hi, Colleen."

Mom came into the living room, carrying a stack of books. "Roger, what happened to you?"

"It's a jungle out there," Casey said.

"Well," she raised her eyebrows, "I hope it doesn't interfere with Dylan's lesson."

Roger scowled. "Dogs come first."

"That's the spirit." She smiled. "I wish I could join you, but the latest Hieronymus the Hamster book needs my attention. Casey, I'll be upstairs in my office if you need me."

"I don't get your mom's business." Roger shook his head and the bandage wobbled. "She publishes kids' books about a hamster, for cryin' out loud. Who cares about a rodent that goes all around the world painting pictures?"

Weird, huh?

"Hey," Casey said, "don't knock it. That hamster makes a fortune. The books sell like crazy."

"It's a hamster."

Exactly.

"Did Mom tell you Dylan is getting his own book series?"

I'm going to be famous.

Roger rolled his eyes. Not very pretty for the purple-and-black one.

"Cranston Pantswick—he's the owner of the largest children's book publishing company. He wrote a story about the dog he had when he was a kid. The dog's name was Scotch Tape. Anyway, Dylan looks like him. Mom's illustrators are doing the artwork. Dylan has publicity photos this week."

I don't even have to paint a picture like that dumb hamster.

"Big deal." Roger tucked his iPad under his arm. "Okay, kid. It's a warm day. Let's go out on the deck and get started."

Casey picked up Dylan's leash and followed him. "This will be fun, Dylan."

Roger is not a fun guy.

"Why on earth am I even here?" Roger grumbled when they got outside. "You don't need private lessons. Waste of my time. I heard you and," he waved his iPad at Dylan, "the short guy, are doing so-so in Agility class."

"Dylan's doing great. Anyway, you're stuck giving us private lessons because my Uncle Rory says you're the best."

Roger scratched at a scab on his chin. "Yeah, I just saw him at Brea PD. The K-9 Unit got a new dog—a Belgian Malinois. Now there's a dog for you." He glared at Dylan. "Doesn't look like some fluffy stuffed animal that belongs on a little girl's bed."

"Did you know my Uncle Rory is *Detective* Lieutenant Kellan now?"

Roger got the hint. "Yeah, I heard something about that."

"What's Dylan doing today?"

Roger ignored him. "Where's his treat bag?"

Casey held out the Ziploc bag.

Roger snatched it away and snorted. "Where are the dog treats, I gave to you?"

"My mom has this thing about crude fiber and refuses to give Dylan commercial dog food. She cooks for him."

Very yummy.

Roger opened the Ziploc bag and sniffed. "This is roast beef!" He looked closer. "All the pieces are the same size."

"Yeah, I think she uses kitchen scissors. She says uniform pieces are better for his digestion."

"Detective Lieutenant Kellan's sister," he muttered. "We'll start with what we learned last week, if you remember anything."

Casey took the treat bag from Roger and waved it in Dylan's direction. "Okay, Little Buddy. We'll show him."

No problem.

"Sit."

Dylan sat.

"Good boy." Casey gave Dylan a treat.

Dylan munched happily while Casey put another treat in his closed hand. "Now we'll do Watch." Slowly, he moved the hand with the treat toward Dylan's face and closer to his nose.

"Watch."

I am! Dylan's eyes never left Casey's closed hand.

"Good boy." Casey gave him the treat.

"Yeah, that's easy." Roger walked in a small circle and came back to them. "What else you got?"

"We've been working on this one." Casey brought two small toys out of his pocket. "Dylan loves his monkey and his rabbit." He showed them to Dylan.

My favorite woobies. Dylan scooted his buns forward and stretched his muzzle out. *They're mine.*

"Not yet, Dylan. Watch."

Dylan kept his eyes on Casey.

Casey held the monkey out. "Take it."

Dylan took the monkey and dropped to his stomach.

"Yeah, so what?" Roger raised his hand to block the sun. "Hurry up. It's getting hot out here."

"For a dog trainer, you could use some patience." Casey turned back to Dylan and held out the rabbit.

Dylan kept the monkey in his mouth but stared at the rabbit. *I want them both.*

Casey brought the rabbit closer to Dylan's mouth.

Dylan wiggled his butt, leaned forward with the monkey still in his mouth, and snuffled the rabbit. *Whine.*

The moment Dylan dropped the monkey, Casey said, "Drop it." When Dylan reached for the rabbit, Casey said, "Take it."

Casey knelt beside Dylan and ruffled his ears. "Good boy! Here's a treat."

Dylan stopped playing with the rabbit long enough to take the treat. He pawed the air. *Aren't you forgetting something?*

Casey laughed. "Right. Two treats."

"Yeah, he did okay."

"Did you know Dylan's working at Children's Hospital now?" Casey stood up. "We wanted to learn Take It and Drop It. Sometimes medication or needles get dropped on the floor and I don't want him to get them. Gotta keep the little guy safe."

"I gotta get out of the sun. Show me the rest inside."

Casey motioned to Dylan. "Heel."

Dylan moved to Casey's left side. Trotting behind Roger, Dylan studied the backs of his ragged tennis shoes. *It would be so easy to nip your ankles.*

In the living room, they went through Stand, Wait, Leave it, and Down. When they finished, Casey showed Dylan the empty bag. "Gone."

Dylan looked at Roger. *Hint, hint.*

"All right. I'm outta here." Roger waggled a scarred hand in the air. "Say goodbye to your mom."

"You know, Dylan did really great today." Casey scooped Dylan up and followed Roger to the door. "It wouldn't kill you to say something nice about him."

"He's not a poodle."

TWO

"Dylan, you're next," called Jean, the trainer at Dream Big K-9 Academy. She checked her iPad. "This is your last test-- the seesaw."

Dylan studied the big wooden seesaw. *Whoever came up with this thing hated dogs.* He planted his buns next to Casey's feet. *The grass tickles, but I don't care. I'm not getting on the seesaw. I don't like it.*

"Dylan," Casey knelt and put his arm around him, "I know you don't like getting on the seesaw," he ruffled Dylan's ears, "but you've got to do it. That's the only way you'll graduate from Agility class."

That's not fair. Dylan turned his face away from Casey. *You can't see me if I'm not looking at you.*

"You've done the seesaw lots of times in Agility class." Casey gently turned Dylan's muzzle toward him. "What's the big deal?"

The seesaw is scary. It moves up and down.

"What about," Casey fished the treat bag out of his shorts pocket and showed it to him. "Double treats?"

Since you put it that way. Dylan padded to where the

end of the seesaw rested on the ground. Slowly he put one paw on the board and then the other. He inched up a bit and looked over his shoulder at Casey.

"Keep going."

Dylan saw Mom on the sidelines. She waved to him, and he sighed.

Dylan saw his and Casey's best friend Sumo holding up his cell phone to get a picture, and he sighed again.

"Look this way, Dylan," yelled Sumo, taking the picture. "We've got to keep Dylan's Dog Squad informed. Your fans want to see you."

This is a lot of pressure. He started to walk, got almost to the middle and the seesaw wobbled. *Agh! It's moving!*

"Go on!" shouted Casey.

Dylan took two more steps and the seesaw dipped. *Yikes!* He hot stepped it to the end of the board and jumped off before it hit the ground. *I'm never doing that again.* He trotted around to Casey and plunked his butt down.

"Good boy." Casey rubbed Dylan's shoulders and gave him two treats. "Let's go graduate."

Dylan and Casey walked over and stood next to Carl and his Bloodhound, Dempsey. Rita grinned and gave them a thumbs up. Joe Friday, her Great Dane, barked.

"You did it." Carl patted Dylan on the head. "I knew you could."

"Congratulations, Agility class," Jean said, getting their attention. "You're graduating from Dream Big K-9 Academy today." She held up a box.

Dylan's eyes popped when he saw her open the box and pull out a bandana.

"The bandana is blue, and it says Dream Big in gold letters." Casey nudged Dylan with his leg. "Aren't you glad you did the seesaw?"

When Jean walked up to Rita, Joe Friday jumped up and put two big paws on Jean's shoulders. "Hey." Rita tried pulling him off, but the big dog stayed put.

"No problem." Jean laughed and put the bandana around his neck.

Jean moved down to Dempsey. He raised his massive head, let his long pink tongue hang out, and offered his paw.

"For you," Jean said, crouching down and tying two bandanas together, "we have to improvise. How much does Dempsey weigh?"

"A hundred and forty pounds. His dad was a hundred and sixty."

She wrapped the bandanas around his neck and patted his head. "Well done."

Carl touched Dempsey's shoulder, put his two hands in the air and twisted them. Dempsey howled happily.

Casey and Jean laughed and said, "Hooray!"

Arf! Dylan agreed.

Jean turned to Casey and Dylan. "You're learning sign language?"

Casey tickled Dylan under his chin. "We've been working on it. Right, Little Buddy?"

Arf!

"Good for you," said Jean. "Sometimes a dog will lose his hearing and if he knows sign language, he won't feel left out. Also," she brought out Dylan's bandana from the box and showed it to him, "there might be situations when it's better not to make a sound. Right, Carl?"

Carl nodded. "In search and rescue, dogs rely on hand signals in tense situations."

Jean knelt and put Dylan's bandana on him. "You've done so well."

Dylan body-bumped Casey. *See my new bandana?*

"We're really sorry the class is over. Dylan had a blast."
Casey looked to Rita and Carl. "I was worried because your
dogs are really big, and he's a little guy."

"Well," Carl caught Jean's eye, "can I tell Casey about
the Catalina K-9 Class? I've already talked to Rita and
she's in."

"Wait a second." She held up one hand. "Casey, your
mom and Sumo are heading this way. I think your mom will
want to hear this."

Dylan tugged on his leash. Casey let it go and Dylan
pranced over to Mom and Sumo. *Notice anything?*

"Good job, Dylan!" Sumo held his cell phone up and
took a picture. "Dream Big! Cool bandana!"

Mom agreed. "You're getting quite the wardrobe."

Dylan wiggled his shoulders and sighed. *I love my
bandanas.*

"Mom, Carl wants to tell us about a new class."

She came closer. "What is it?"

"It's a one-day class on Catalina Island," Carl began.

"Oh, wow, Catalina!" Sumo jumped in. "Remember
what happened when we went camping?"

"We had so much fun," Casey finished for him and shot
a look at his mom.

"Uh, yeah," Sumo clammed up.

Carl eyed the boys and snickered. "Our group is small--
four handlers and their dogs. We'll take the Catalina
Express, get there about eleven o'clock and leave around five
o'clock. Dogs are required to be in a crate while on the boat,
but I have a collapsible one Dylan can use."

What's a boat?

"There are some other requirements," Carl continued.
"Dylan has to have proof of vaccinations. I imagine he has
that since he came from South Korea."

Mom nodded. "I can email that to you."

"Is Dylan chipped?"

Chipped? Dylan looked himself all over. *I'm not broken.* Dylan pawed Casey's leg.

Casey touched Dylan's neck. "Remember when we went to Dr. Adams, and he injected the microchip here?"

I was scared.

"The chip is important because it has all your information." Casey tapped the spot again. "If you ever get lost, a veterinarian can read the chip and get you home to me."

I'll never be lost. Dylan rubbed against Casey's leg. *We're buddies.*

"That's right," agreed Carl. "People always think their house door will never get left open, or their pet will never lose its collar. Good pet owners lose pets, too."

"That's sad," Sumo said.

Mom had her cell phone out and was taking notes. "What will Casey need to bring?"

"Not much. Snacks, lunch, and water are provided for him and Dylan. Casey will need a compass app on his cell phone. I can email the rest of the list to you tonight."

"Can we, Mom?"

This sounds fun. Especially the part about snacks.

"Is this like bow-wow boot camp?" Sumo interrupted. "Will Casey and Dylan track buffalo, forage for food, eat wild bugs, and boil water from a stream to drink?"

Mom laughed. "You're wasting your time with social media, Sumo. You should write fiction."

Sumo's face went red. "Just asking."

"Catalina K-9 Class is for owners who have a special bond with their dog. We do a little bit of everything. Hand and audio commands, agility, and even some search and rescue techniques." Carl paused. "Roger Bennett recommended you and Dylan. I agreed."

Casey's mouth dropped open. "Roger? The grumpy old guy that doesn't like people and thinks Dylan isn't a dog because he's short?"

"I keep telling you," Jean said, "Roger thinks Dylan has potential. He's certain Dylan can become a certified working dog, and Roger is never wrong." She shrugged. "It's up to you if you want to invest the time."

All eyes went to the exercise field where handlers and German Shepherds, Golden Retrievers, Labradors, and Great Danes were running around and working on skills.

All eyes shifted back to Dylan.

Dylan wiggled his shoulders and tried checking out his new bandana. *My ears are too curly. They're getting in the way.* He gave his head a shake and his ears fluffed out. Dylan looked up at Casey from under his long eyelashes. *What?*

"Are any other kids going?" Casey asked. "I don't want to be the only kid. That'd be boring."

"It's always been with adults," Carl admitted. "Do you want to go Colleen? It's this Friday."

Casey snorted. "Are you kidding? Mom's idea of hiking is walking around the Brea Mall."

She gave Casey The Look. "Gee, Carl, I wish I could. I have a big meeting on Friday with my illustrators for two Hieronymus the Hamster books." She heaved a sigh. "We have a new book coming out for Christmas and we're planning another one right after." Another sigh. "You know how it is in the children's book business—busy, busy, busy!"

"I don't want to go alone. All old people talk about is their aches and pains and what it was like when they were a kid."

Sumo laughed. "Like they can even remember that far back."

"Hey," Casey brightened, "can Sumo come?"

Carl hesitated. "It's short notice. Your mom would have to let me know tonight."

"No problem," Sumo grinned. "She's busy planning stuff. She's getting married again."

"Who is it this time," Jean asked.

"The guy from Paso Robles. He's got a winery and has tons of money."

Mom raised her cell phone. "Send me everything you need. I'll work out the details with Sumo's mom and get back to you tonight."

Casey and Sumo high-fived each other.

"Hear that, Little Buddy? We're going to Catalina Island."

Arf!

THREE

"Did you really forget to tell your mom about Tabitha, Tanya, and Tori's birthday party?" Sumo asked.

Dylan wiggled his buns. *Birthday parties are fun. Since they are triplets, their party will be really fun.*

Casey shrugged. "You know how snoopy Mom is. She'd want to know when and where it is, and what they're serving for food. She'd have a fit if she knew their parents hired Taco Man to cater the party."

I like tacos.

"All the kids have Taco Man at their birthday parties. It's like a law or something."

"Yeah, except me. Remember my party? I'm the only kid on the planet to have stir fry and kale salad. The only reason I had a birthday cake was because Mom baked it herself."

"Aw, lighten-up. Your mom cares about you."

I like cake. Did you get ice cream?

Casey went to his closet and took out his backpack. "Help me find their gifts." He looked around. "Where did I put them?"

Look under your bed. That's where everything is.

"It was hard to come up with gift ideas for three girls." Sumo moved a T-shirt off a chair and tossed it onto the floor. "What did you get them?"

Casey got on his hands and knees, looked under his bed, and pulled out a baseball.

Told you.

"You gotta be kidding."

I'm with Sumo on this one.

Casey rolled the ball between his fingers. "What's wrong with a baseball?"

"They're triplets! They're girly girls! You're giving them one measly baseball?"

"Nah." Casey shoved some papers aside on his desk and found two more balls. "One for each of them." He dropped them into his backpack and zipped it up.

"Dude. Aren't you going to wrap them?"

Casey made a face. "Why? They're just going to play with them."

Dylan flicked his ears and looked away. *Even I know you're supposed to wrap gifts for girls.*

"C'mon. Let's go."

"What are you going to say when your mom asks where we're going?"

Casey hefted the backpack. "I'll tell her we're going to play ball."

Oh-oh.

"Isn't that kind of like lying?"

"Nah. It's not a lie because I don't mean it, so it doesn't count."

Yeah, it does.

Casey started down the hall but slowed when he heard voices coming from his mom's office. He turned around to face Dylan, raised both hands and extended his left palm up. Quickly he brought his right hand down to his left palm at a right angle. "Stop."

Dylan stopped and Sumo plowed into him.

Yip!

"Sorry, Dylan." Sumo backed up.

Casey whispered, "You really need to learn sign language."

"It's too hard."

Dylan grinned up at Sumo. *I'm learning it!*

"Just be quiet." Casey tip-toed into Mom's office ahead of Sumo and Dylan.

"Of course, I know it's important, Cranston." Mom swiveled in her chair and gave a little hand wave to them. Turning back to her computer, she said, "Have I ever let you down?"

Cranston leaned forward in his chair, his wrinkly face filling the computer screen. "When I asked Sasha to shoot Dylan's pictures a day early, she happily agreed. She didn't quibble, so why should you?"

"That's because you've got lots of money," she said under her breath.

"What?"

She threw her hands up in the air. "I'm not quibbling. I'm trying to tell you Dylan's appointment with the groomer will need to be changed to today. I'm not sure I can do that on such short notice."

Cranston sat back in his chair and steepled his gnarly fingers. "We won't know until we try, will we?"

Mom's lips flattened. "I'll get back to you."

The old man's face grinned in triumph. "I knew I could count on you."

"Of course." Her voice tried for cheerful, but her index

finger hit End Meeting on her computer before she'd
finished speaking.

"Why do you let him boss you around like that, Ms. D?"

She pushed away from her desk and reached down to
pet Dylan. "Whoever has the gold makes the rules."

"Huh?"

"Johnny Hart," Casey said. "He was a cartoonist."

What's a cartoonist?

"Cranky Pants signed two of Mom's illustrators to do
the illustrations for Dylan's book," Casey said. "We're
talking big bucks."

"Oh."

Mom reached for her cell phone. "Hold on, guys. Let
me make this call." She found the contact for Happy Paws
and said, "Hi Pamela, it's Colleen. Is it possible to move
Dylan's grooming appointment to today? Something has
come up." She listened. "Great. I'll bring Dylan over in an
hour. Thanks so much."

She disconnected and turned to Casey. "I have a
meeting this afternoon. I need you to pick Dylan up from
Happy Paws for me."

Why do I have to get washed all over for some pictures?
Dylan looked at his blond feet tinged with dirt. He licked
some Cheetos dust on his fur. *I look good to me.*

"Uh," Casey began.

Mom went on alert. "Is there a problem? What were
you two planning on doing?"

Casey raised his backpack. "Play some ball?"

She studied him. "Where?"

Oh-oh. This is getting complicated.

"Carbon Canyon Park."

Mom reached for a stack of photographs on her desk.
"I'll ask Pamela to text you when Dylan is finished. He

usually takes a couple of hours." She started sorting the pictures. "Plenty of time for you to play ball."

"But."

"This is really important." She tossed the photos aside. "You've got to keep Dylan clean. His photo shoot for his book is tomorrow."

"I know."

She held up one hand. "This is really, really important. Please carry Dylan out of Happy Paws and put him into his bike trailer. Don't let him walk on the asphalt—it will make his paws dirty. He's got to be really, really..."

"...clean. Got it."

Her shoulders slumped. "I'm sorry. Cranston is being difficult. All these changes at the last minute. If this book deal wasn't so important, I'd tell him no."

Grr. He's grumpy.

"You're right, Dylan." She glanced at her cell phone. "It's almost lunchtime. I'll make us grilled cheese sandwiches."

Arf! I love cheese.

"There's a happy vote. Hurry up and wash your hands. See you downstairs in fifteen minutes."

FOUR

"Hi guys." Pamela waved to them from behind the counter at Happy Paws. "Casey, your mom called."

Casey came closer and held up his cell phone. "Keep Dylan clean, right?"

Whine. Dylan wiggled his buns and some pens rolled off the counter.

"Right."

Sumo brought his cell phone out of his pocket. "Dylan, look this way. Dylan's Dog Squad wants to know what you're doing."

Pamela laughed. "I follow Dylan on social media. He has a better life than I do."

"Sumo keeps everybody informed." Casey rubbed Dylan between his ears. "Why is Dylan on the counter?"

Pamela shrugged. "After his grooming, I started to put him in a crate, but he said he wanted to be up front."

Sumo smirked. "Dylan said that?"

Pamela stammered, "Something like that."

Dylan licked Pamela's cheek. *I like seeing everybody when they come in.*

Casey sniffed and looked around. "What's that smell?"

Pamela brushed Dylan's topknot out of his eyes. "Your mom wanted Dylan to have a blueberry facial today."

Sumo and Casey made faces.

Dylan shook his ears and his topknot flopped into his eyes again. *Smells yummy.*

"Whew," Sumo waved a hand in front of his face. "He smells like blueberry pie."

"He's got to look good for his photo shoot tomorrow." Pamela brushed Dylan's topknot away from his eyes again. "Dylan's so cute. No wonder he's getting his own book series."

"Let's go, Little Buddy." Casey tucked him under one arm and gave Pamela a wave. "Thanks!"

Outside, Casey unzipped the front screen on Dylan's bike trailer and helped him into it. "Everybody from school will be at the party today."

Dylan turned in a circle on his cushion, plopped down and looked out the side screen. He liked the way the wind blew in and brought all kinds of smells.

When they got to Carbon Canyon Park, Dylan felt the bike slow. He pushed his snout against the front screen and saw kids everywhere. One sniff told him Taco Man was already here. *Maybe he needs my help!*

Casey unzipped the front screen and let Dylan out. "Hold still." He attached Dylan's leash to his collar and looked around. "Do you see Tabitha, Tanya, and Tori?"

"Nuh-uh," Sumo slipped his backpack on. "But Jake and the others are over there."

"Great. This will be so much fun." Casey picked up his backpack. "Remember Dylan, you've got to stay clean or we're dead."

Dead doesn't sound like fun.

"Hey, listen!" Sumo pointed. "They have a mariachi band. Awesome."

Dylan looked. In front of the duck pond, he saw men wearing fancy shirts and big hats. *I wish I had a hat like that.* Dylan tipped his head left and right. His ears flopped left and right. *How do hats stay on?* Loud, happy music blared out and he wiggled his butt. Ducks were everywhere and they were wiggling their butts, too. They strutted around on flat feet, making honking noises. *Duck music!*

"Okay, Little Buddy. You've got to remember. You can't chase the ducks."

Who me?

Casey pointed to the sign. "It says, 'Do Not Chase the Ducks.' You'll get dirty and then Mom will kill us."

You're really taking the fun out of today.

Casey jiggled Dylan's leash. "Let's find the gift table, drop off the gifts for the girls, and go get tacos."

Sumo started walking. "I'm starving. Want to have a taco eating contest? I bet I can eat ten."

Me, too.

They passed a pretty table decorated with balloons. Dylan slowed and lifted his head up to see three birthday cakes and too many cupcakes to count. *Wow! That's a lot of cake.*

"They always have red velvet birthday cakes with cream cheese frosting," Casey said.

I love cream cheese.

Sumo pointed to the cupcakes on the table. "Look at all the different cupcakes. My favorites are the ones with sprinkles."

A square table under a big tree was decorated with more balloons and piled high with gifts tied with ribbons and bows. Sumo put three boxes from Kay's Jewelers on the table, and Casey pulled the three baseballs out of his backpack.

"How are they going to know they're from you?" Sumo asked.

Casey stared at him. "Who else would give them baseballs?"

Dylan flicked his ears. *Exactly.*

Casey, Dylan, and Sumo got in line for Taco Man. After filling his plate with tacos, Casey led Dylan to a long table with more food. Dylan got on his hind legs, put his paws on the table and snuffled left and right on the white paper tablecloth.

"Hold on," Casey said. "I'm getting you some tomatoes, cheese and avocado." Casey put them on another plate and dumped something out of a wicker basket. "These are tortilla chips." He held one out in front of Dylan.

Dylan sniffed it, licked it, and gulped it down. *Salty.*

"Hey, he likes them." Sumo held out a chip to Dylan. "Here you go."

Dylan flopped his tongue up and down. *Thirsty.*

Casey looked around again. "I still don't see the girls."

"They're probably doing girl things. Anyway, there's a ton of kids. Let's eat and then try to find them."

"Casey! Sumo!" Jake waved to them. "There's room here."

"Okay." Casey balanced their plates with his right hand and used his left hand to steer Dylan on his leash toward a picnic table with a bunch of kids.

Four rabbits hopped out of the bushes. They paused in front of them, ears straight in the air, and twitching their noses.

Dylan pulled on his leash. *What are they?*

"Check out Dylan." Sumo grabbed Casey's arm. "Has he ever seen a rabbit before?"

"They're rabbits, Dylan," Casey explained. "Just like your woobie."

Dylan stared. *My woobie doesn't hop.* Dylan took a step forward and his back quivered.

The rabbits flicked their ears and sprang into the bushes.

"C'mon." Casey dragged Dylan away, to Jake's picnic table. "Hi, everybody!" The other kids scooted down to make room. Casey put their plates of food on the table and swung his long legs over the bench.

Dylan started to sit but the grass tickled his buns. *Arf!*

"Okay, Little Buddy." Casey put Dylan next to him on the bench. "Don't tell Mom but you can sit here. Got to keep you clean."

There's that word again.

"Don't wiggle or you'll fall off."

This party has a lot of rules. Dylan sat up straight, put both paws on the table and looked at their plates. *Ready.*

"Nice try." Casey nudged his paws off the table and put a plate of grilled beef, tomatoes, cheese, and avocado in front of him.

Dylan dove in, but Casey quickly grabbed his shoulders. *Hey!*

"Sorry. You're getting cheese in your ears." Casey held Dylan's ears back with one hand and picked up his taco with his other hand. "Now try it."

Dylan leaned forward and nibbled. *Feels weird.*

When Dylan polished off his food, he looked at Casey's clean plate. He leaned around Casey to check out Sumo. Sumo had two plates in front of him. He'd finished one and was working on a second plate loaded with tacos and chow. *I don't get it. The kid's skinny, comes up to Casey's chin, but he can pack it away. Next time, I'm sitting next to him.*

"Hi, Casey and Sumo," chorused Tabitha, Tanya, and Tori.

"Hi," Casey said.

"Hi." Sumo waved a taco in their direction and swallowed. "Awesome party."

Dylan blinked at the girls. *I can never tell you apart.*

They came closer and petted Dylan. "You smell like blueberries."

You talk at the same time. Crazy.

"We're glad you made it," Tabitha or Tanya or Tori said.

"Yeah, Tanya," Casey made a face, "sorry we were late. Dylan had an appointment at the groomer."

How do you know it's Tanya? Dylan snuffled Casey's plate for crumbs.

One of them said, "Hurry up, Sumo, and come over."

The other one said, "We're going to do the piñata."

"Oh wow," Sumo said, shoveling food into his mouth. "Count me in."

Casey rubbed Dylan's back. "Have you ever seen a piñata before?"

Dylan watched Casey's mouth move up and down when he said piñata. *That's a strange word.*

They dumped their trash and went over to a big circle of kids. One boy was in the middle of the circle, holding a baseball bat. A girl tied a blindfold over his eyes. Under a big tree another girl was holding one end of a rope. The other end hung over a tree branch, and something dangled from it.

I don't get it.

Casey bent down to Dylan and pointed at the thing in

the air. "That's a piñata. It looks like a toy donkey but inside it's full of candy and prizes.

Strange but yummy idea.

"Brandon, he's the kid with the baseball bat and blindfold. He's going to swing the bat and try to hit the piñata. Jennifer, she's the girl holding the rope, will pull the rope up and down, making the piñata swing and move."

Sumo laughed. "It's fun to watch the kid with the bat running all over, trying to hit the piñata. There's always a lot of yelling and laughing."

"When the piñata gets hit hard enough, it'll break open. Kids race in and get the candy and prizes. It's fun. Everyone at the party gets three swings with the bat."

Everyone? Dylan looked at his furry paws. *Even me?*

The kids started shouting and Brandon started swinging the bat. He clobbered the piñata but no luck. A girl with yellow curls went at it, and the crowd started screaming, "Go Monica!"

"That's Monica the Maniac," Sumo knelt close to Dylan. "When we were little, she was on our tee ball team. She whacked the ball off the tee and then knocked the tee twenty feet across the field with her follow up."

"Gotta admire her swing," Casey said. "I heard she plays golf now."

Dylan moved closer to Casey.

After a dozen kids, the donkey piñata was dying a slow death on the end of the rope—but no candy, no prizes.

"Casey," Jake shouted, "get over here and get us some candy."

Casey shrugged and handed Dylan's leash to Sumo. "Be right back."

Sumo got his cell phone out and stuck the end of Dylan's leash in his pocket. Casey went into the circle.

Tabitha or Tori or Tanya tied the blindfold around Casey's eyes. Tabitha or Tori or Tanya spun him around three times.

"Hey, not so fast! I'm getting dizzy."

"Casey!" "Casey!" "Casey!"

Dylan's stomach growled and he looked around. The table with the party balloons and birthday cakes wasn't far away. *When is it cake time?*

"Casey," Sumo shouted, holding his cell phone up, "I'm getting this on video."

Dylan's stomach growled again. *Hurry up, Casey. I'm getting hungry.*

Dylan looked at the cakes, looked at Casey, and then looked at Sumo. *No one's looking at me, so why not?*

Dylan backed up, letting his leash fall slowly out of Sumo's pocket.

"Hit it, Casey!" "We want candy!"

The cake table was even better close-up. Dylan stood on his hind legs, put his paws on the table and inched toward the cakes. The tablecloth bunched up and the cakes and cupcakes slid around. *This is good.*

Dylan tried harder. He pawed at the first cake, but it was too far back. *Rats!* The second cake was a little closer, but not quite. Dylan sidled down the table to the third cake and worked the tablecloth with his paws. *Almost!* He stuck his tongue out, lunged forward, and his back feet slipped out. *Agh!* He fell face-first into the cake and frosting gunked up his snout. *Was it really cream cheese frosting?* He shot out his pink tongue and licked some frosting off. *Yup! Casey was right.* He pawed at the cake, and it slid off the table, breaking apart on the grass.

Dylan dropped down to all fours and gobbled up the pieces. *Red velvet cake is yummy.*

A rustle came from the bushes. Dylan lifted his head

and a blur of rabbits raced past him, disappearing into the trees. *They want to play!* Dylan wiggled his butt. *Me, too. Arf! Arf!*

He started after them but skidded to a stop.

Casey said not to chase the ducks.

Dylan sat back on his buns and scratched his ear. *Hmm.* He looked over and saw Casey haul back and whack the donkey piñata. The donkey's head flew off and its body broke apart, spilling out candy and prizes. The kids pounced on the stuff, laughing, and shoving.

Poor donkey. Dylan shuddered. *Yikes.*

Two more bunnies hopped by Dylan. Their noses twitched; their ears pointed straight up. Dylan tried twitching his nose. *Feels funny.*

Dylan went back to Casey and the kids. They were going crazy, unwrapping candy, and having a good time. *Nothing for me to do over there.* Dylan snuffled the ground hoping for red velvet cake crumbs. *Nothing for me to do here. Even the cake is gone. Sigh.*

Dylan got to his hind legs, put his paws on the table and two-stepped it up and down the table. He swiped at a cupcake, but it was too far away. Dylan slid down to the ground.

A bunny bounced by.

Casey said not to chase the ducks but... he didn't say anything about chasing rabbits!

Arf! Dylan turned and raced after the bunny. *Wait for me!*

FIVE

"*What* did you do?"

Nothing.

"You put your face in the birthday cake!"

Did not. Dylan stuck his tongue out and up and licked off a glop of frosting on his black nose. *Maybe just a little.* He pawed Casey's knee, sighing happily. *You were right. It's cream cheese frosting.*

"Mom's going to kill me," Casey moaned. "You've got red velvet cake smooshed in your ears. You're filthy."

Dylan looked down at himself. *Just the front of me. That's not so bad.*

Casey pulled twigs and leaves out of Dylan's topknot and ears.

Ow!

Sumo came up and hooked a thumb over his shoulder. "I've brought Tabitha, Tanya, and Tori."

"Why?"

"Oh, you poor baby!" Tabitha and Tanya and Tori cooed, dropping to their knees. They held Dylan's face in their hands and looked him over. "You could've been hurt."

Dylan's big brown eyes peeked up at them from under his long eyelashes. *Try telling that to Casey.*

Sumo rolled his eyes. "They're girls. They know about hair and stuff."

"Who cares?" Casey waved his hands in the air. "My mom's going to kill me dead. Dylan has his photo shoot tomorrow." He checked his cell phone. "Happy Paws is closed. There's no time to get him clean."

"I have an idea," Tabitha or Tanya or Tori said.

"What, Tabitha?"

Dylan studied the three girls. *What's different about you?* He gave up and shook his ears. Red velvet cake crumbs rained down and he licked them up. *Casey probably guesses.*

"While everyone is eating the candy from the piñata," Tabitha turned to her sisters, "we'll take Dylan to our house." She pointed to a two-story house across the street. "We'll get him cleaned up."

"Your mom will never know," Tanya or Tori said.

Sumo shrugged. "What have you got to lose?"

"Okay," Casey looked over to the party, "what about your mom? Won't she wonder where you went?"

Tori or Tanya said, "We already told her we wanted to go home and change our shoes."

"Shoes?" Casey thought about that one.

Sumo jumped in. "Don't try to figure it out. Just go with it."

"Okay. Thanks." He picked Dylan up and started walking after Tanya, Tabitha, and Tori. "No blabbing any of this to Mom, got it, Little Buddy?"

Dylan hooked his muzzle over Casey's shoulder and watched the birthday cake table disappear. *Are we coming back for cake?*

They crossed the street and went to a house with geraniums around the mailbox. Tanya and Tori and Tabitha led the way to the front door and let everybody in.

"You and Sumo can wait in the living room. We'll be back before you know it."

Casey handed Dylan over. "Be a good boy."

That's me.

When the girls and Dylan left, Casey said, "I can't believe they're not mad at Dylan for wrecking the birthday cake."

"They still have two cakes left and a ton of cupcakes. Besides, Dylan's the coolest dog. Everybody likes him." Sumo plopped onto the white couch and put his feet on the coffee table. "I think it's kind of funny."

Casey collapsed into a chair, laid his head back, and rolled it from side-to-side. "That's because you're not the one my mom is going to kill dead."

"She won't. Your mom's cool."

"Cranky Pants is putting a lot of pressure on her. If Mom loses this book deal, it'll be my fault."

"Not going to happen. Tanya, Tabitha, and Tori are girls. They have," Sumo put his fingers in his hair and moved them around, "shampoo, smelly stuff, and hair dryers. They can fix it."

Casey turned to look at him. "You think so?"

"Yeah. My mom is always messing around with that stuff."

"How long does it take," Casey waved his hands around his head, "to do all that?" He checked his cell phone. "It's four o'clock. We've got to be home by six."

"Relax. They've got this."

Casey sat straight up. "You're staying for dinner, right?"

Sumo grinned. "Depends if your mom kills you dead or not."

Casey got up and grabbed the remote for the TV. "Angels are playing the Toronto Blue Jays."

"Okay."

At the end of the first inning, Casey checked his cell phone again. "What's taking so long? It's been twenty-five minutes."

"Ta-da!" Tanya and Tabitha and Tori squealed.

Dylan ran into the living room and jumped onto Casey's lap.

"Hey, Little Buddy!" Casey held him at arm's length and studied him. "You're clean."

I miss the crumbs.

Casey looked at the girls. "How did you do it?"

They smiled. "We're geniuses!"

"Told you so," Sumo said. He got up and pulled his cell phone out of his pocket. "Over here, Dylan." He took a couple of pictures. "Social media, here you come."

Casey and Dylan got out of the chair. "I'm sorry about your birthday cake."

Tanya or Tori or Tabitha waved it off. "There's plenty."

"Poor Dylan," Tanya or Tori or Tabitha said, "had a little tummy ache but he's feeling better now."

"Oh, man." Casey rolled his eyes. "Don't tell me you ralphed up the cake."

Dylan faced Casey. *Burp.*

"Let's go get some cake." Sumo rubbed his stomach. "I'm starving."

They walked across the street and over to the party. The kids were already crowded around the birthday cake table, holding paper plates and plastic forks.

"About time!" "Hurry up!" "Cut the cakes!"

"Girls!" Their mom saw them and smiled. "We've been waiting to light the candles. Time to make a wish."

Casey scooped Dylan up and followed Sumo to the table. Tanya, Tabitha, and Tori squeezed through the kids and waited until all the birthday candles were lit.

Whine. Dylan snuggled closer to Casey. *The cakes are on fire.*

"It's okay, Little Buddy."

The mariachi band launched into "Happy Birthday" and all the kids joined in. When the singing stopped, the girls locked arms, leaned forward, and blew out all the candles.

Where did the fire go?

"Wait here, Casey. I'll be back."

They watched Sumo grab a paper plate and join the kids in line. Casey hugged Dylan. "We'll have a party when it's your birthday."

Really? Wow.

Tanya, Tabitha, and Tori got busy cutting the cakes and putting slices on the paper plates. Some of the kids added a cupcake. Sumo came back with cake and two cupcakes.

Casey snagged a vanilla cupcake with sprinkles from Sumo's plate.

"Hey! That's my favorite."

"You always go back for seconds." Casey put Dylan down, broke off a bit of cupcake and held it out to him. "You've had enough red velvet cake, Little Buddy."

You sound like Mom.

Sumo inhaled a cupcake, licked the wrapper, and then waved it toward the street. "Your mom's coming."

"No!"

"See for yourself."

Casey pulled Dylan close to him, flapped his ears up and down and brushed crumbs off his face.

"Hi, Ms. D."

"Hi, Sumo." She waited.

"Mom. Hi." Casey straightened up. "Funny seeing you here."

She gave him a patient smile before waving to Tanya, Tabitha, and Tori's mom. "The girls have their birthday party at Carbon Canyon Park on the second Saturday in July every year."

"Oh, yeah."

Really? Dylan pawed Casey's leg. *You didn't think about that?*

Mom changed the subject by picking Dylan up. "Everything go okay at Happy Paws?"

"Yeah. Great."

"Pamela did a wonderful job." She fingered Dylan's curly ears. "I'm amazed you were able to keep him clean at the park."

"Well," Casey stood straighter, "you told me to keep him clean and that's what I did. Anything to help. Right, Little Buddy?"

Uh.

She snuggled Dylan to her. "It was probably silly for Dylan to get a blueberry facial, but tomorrow is a big day."

"Yeah."

She brought her face close to Dylan's, sniffed and pulled away. "Why does he smell like wildflowers?"

SIX

Sumo held the front door of Brea Police Department open. Casey and Dylan pushed past him and went over to the front desk. Casey heaved two shopping bags onto the counter. "Hi Lisa. Is Uncle Rory here?"

"Hi, guys. Casey, you just missed Lieutenant Kellan. He took a team of cadets to the Brea Community Theatre."

Arf!

"Hi, Dylan. Are you ready for your photo shoot?"

Arf! Arf!

Lisa checked her iPad. "Cranston Pantswick and your mom are already at the Brea Community Theatre. The photographer arrived thirty minutes ago and should be set up. This is so exciting." Cadet Chen giggled. "I know a celebrity."

Sumo raised his cell phone. "Social media is all over this. You can't believe how many hits Dylan gets every day. Dylan's Dog Squad will be there if you need help with crowd control."

"Thanks, Sumo." Cadet Chen kept her smile to herself. "If Lieutenant Kellan needs help from Dylan's Dog Squad,

I'm sure he'll ask." She opened the shopping bags, closed her eyes, and inhaled. "Pumpkin bread?"

"My mom baked it this morning. She's really stressed out about Dylan's photo shoot. Cranky Pants is never happy."

Cadet Chen put a small hand over her heart. "I love it when your mom gets stressed out and bakes." She blushed. "Sorry, you know what I mean. When *Hieronymus the Hamster Goes to Egypt* was coming out, we got a different cheesecake every day for a week."

What's cheesecake?

Casey nodded. "The photo shoot was supposed to be just Dylan. Two days ago, Cranky Pants decided to include a kid. He said it would be 'excellent publicity'."

"Ms. D is really freaked out because he's always changing his mind at the last minute," Sumo said.

"Then he decided it would be 'excellent publicity' to use a kid from the Brea Community Theatre for a model."

Excellent publicity are his favorite words.

"I know." Cadet Chen slid a look to Captain Rizzoli's closed door. She tossed her long black braid over her shoulder, leaned forward on her elbows, and whispered, "Captain Rizzoli had to move several things around. She wasn't happy about it." She checked her iPad again. "Is it true thirty boys are auditioning for the part?"

"Cranky Pants wants to find a kid that looks like him when he was a boy."

Sumo snorted. "Like you could find some dorky kid who wears loafers and bow ties."

What are loafers and bow ties?

Cadet Chen laughed. "This is California—home of Hollywood and Disneyland. If anyone can find a mini-Cranston Pantswick, Ms. Donovan can. She's amazing."

"Yeah. C'mon, Dylan. Let's go make you a star."

"I'll take the pumpkin bread to the kitchen," she called after them.

"Thanks."

I bet she takes a nibble.

Outside Casey picked up Dylan and headed toward the elevator. "We'll take the elevator down to the Brea Community Theatre. If you get dirty now, Mom will kill me."

Can I get dirty after?

"How long is this going to take?" Sumo's thumbs tapped his cell phone. "Dylan's Dog Squad wants to know. They're already here."

"This is the first time Mom is working with Sasha the photographer. Dylan," Casey hugged him, "is very photogenic. But no telling about the dopey kid they find to be Cranston."

The elevator doors opened.

"Whoa," Casey and Sumo said together.

Sumo's thumbs stopped midair above his cell phone. "This is a lot of kids."

"Gotta be a hundred."

I can only count to three.

Casey, Dylan, and Sumo pushed through the crowd of boys and moms. A group of cadets were studying iPads and getting instructions from Lieutenant Kellan.

Casey waited until they were through. "Hey, Uncle Rory. How's it going?"

Rory waved the cadets off and turned around. He smiled when he saw them but rubbed his forehead. "Cranston Pantswick is a lot of work. I can't believe he had a dog when he was a boy—let alone wrote a story about him."

Casey laughed. "That's why they call it fiction."

"You sound like your mom." Rory nodded. "Hi, Sumo." He reached down to Dylan. "Are you ready for your job?"

Arf! My job is to keep clean.

"With you on the cover, the book will be a hit." Rory straightened up. "That reminds me." He pointed to a woman with chin-length brown hair putting up a backdrop. She was surrounded by a group of people, all wearing Dylan's Dog Squad T-shirts. "That's Sasha, the photographer. I'm supposed to tell you to check in with her."

"Okay. Can you tell Mom we're here?"

"She's with Cranston." Rory made a face. "I've had enough of him. I'll send her a text."

"Chicken."

Chicken? Dylan looked around. *Where?*

Casey motioned to Sumo, and they worked their way over to the photographer.

"Hi. I'm Casey. That's Sumo and this is Dylan."

Arf!

She took something silver off her Sony camera and slipped it into her cargo pants pocket. "Hi, I'm Sasha." She studied Sumo. "Are you a model?"

Sumo scowled. "What? No way."

"Social media is his thing." Casey gestured to the people surrounding her in Dylan's Dog Squad T-shirts. "I see you've already met Dylan's fans."

"They've been telling me wild stories about Dylan." She tickled Dylan's muzzle. "He was dognapped and helped the police catch the bad guys." She brought her face close to his. "Good boy!"

Casey and my friends helped.

"They also said he works for Children's Hospital and the Read to Me Program. That's a lot for one pup." She turned Dylan's face from side-to-side. "You're really cute. I can see why you're getting your own book."

Better than that dumb old Hieronymus the hamster.

"Dylan just graduated from Agility class," Sumo added. "Tomorrow we're going to Catalina Island for the Catalina K-9 Class." He brought out his cell phone. "I'm going, too. Got to keep social media informed."

She laughed. "Maybe you'll be White House Press Secretary someday."

Sumo blushed but shrugged it off. "Social media is fun."

Sasha clapped her hands together. "Let's get to work. Casey, will Dylan pose for me?"

"Sure. Just tell him what to do. He's very smart."

Whine. Thanks, Casey.

"All pet owners say that. I could tell you stories." Sasha rolled her eyes. "I had one pet mom who was convinced her Maltese could play chess."

"Too slow. Dylan likes roulette."

Sasha's eyebrows went up.

Casey laughed. "Just kidding. Tell him what you want, and he'll do it. Right, Little Buddy?"

Dylan nudged Casey. *Did you bring the treat bag?*

Casey took the Ziploc bag out of his shorts pocket and waved it.

Show time!

Sasha put Dylan on a chair, then on a table, and changed the background on the backdrop several times. "I'm getting pictures of Dylan in different poses. Gina Capaldi and Priscilla Burris, the illustrators, can adapt the photos to fit the story."

Dylan's Dog Squad waved to Dylan and called out. "Dylan!" "Looking good!" "You're famous."

This isn't so hard. Dylan liked being outside. Sasha was

nice and Casey kept the treats coming. After a while, his stomach rumbled. *I'm getting a little full.*

Sasha's cell phone vibrated, and she checked it. "Mr. Pantswick and your mom want us to come over." She raised up on tiptoes, trying to see over the crowd. "Maybe he's found a boy."

Casey hooked Dylan's leash to his collar. "What about this stuff?"

"Hmm." She chewed on her bottom lip. "I can't just leave it here."

Sumo called over to Dylan's Dog Squad. "Can you watch this for us?" Hands waved and heads nodded.

"Great. Thanks." She grabbed a backpack and loaded her camera equipment. "Ready."

When they got closer, they could see Cranston glaring at Mom.

"Oh-oh," Sasha said. "That means he didn't find a boy." She sighed. "Cranston can be a little difficult."

"Why do you put up with him," asked Sumo.

She cocked her head and smiled. "I'm his daughter."

"Get out!" Casey and Sumo said together.

Get out!

She shook her head. "Yup. Lucky me. Let's get this over with."

Cranston ignored them. Instead, he threw his skinny arms into the air, collapsed into a chair, and swung a bony right leg over his left. The crease in his trousers stayed razor sharp. He tapped his left loafer on the concrete and its tassel bounced. "Waste of time," he snapped. "Ninety-eight boys and not one of them worthy to be me." Beady black eyes under bushy white eyebrows locked on Mom. "You told me you'd take care of this."

"Hi, Mom."

She took a deep breath, then managed a smile in their direction. "How did it go?"

"Great!" Sasha held up her camera and came closer. "Dylan's a natural. I got some terrific shots, head, body, and background. I think your illustrators will be pleased."

"At least one thing went right," Cranston grumbled. He twisted an oversized watch around and around on his wrist. "Of course, it was up to *me* to discover the perfect dog to be Scotch Tape." A long finger shot out. "Colleen, why can't you find me a boy?"

"Why can't you be nice?" Sumo blurted out. "No wonder people call you Cranky Pants!"

The old man's head swiveled around on his long neck.

"Sumo!" Mom gasped. "I'm sorry Cranston." She put her hands out in front of her like she was trying to soothe a crying kid.

"You. Come here."

Sumo stayed where he was.

"Cranston, this is my son Casey and, well, you've just met his friend Sumo."

"Sasha," the old man waved his hand toward Sumo, "get some shots."

Sasha brought her camera up and started moving around Sumo, snapping pictures. She looked at something on the camera, moved something on the camera, and came around to Cranston's side. She handed him the camera. "What do you think?"

Cranston pursed his thin lips. He looked at something on the camera, moved something on the camera, handed the camera back to Sasha, and said to Sumo. "You'll do."

"Uh-uh." Sumo backed away. "I *do* social media. I'm not *in* social media."

Mom interrupted. "Please, Sumo. This is an important

book deal." She smiled sweetly. "It's just for the cover of the book. That's it."

"Aw, Ms. D. I don't want to be a model. The kids will make fun of me. No one I know is a model."

I'm a model.

Mom raised her eyebrows. "Do you still want to go to Catalina Island with Casey and Dylan tomorrow?"

"Ms. D, this is blackmail."

She smiled. "Absolutely."

Casey punched Sumo in the arm. "You're gonna look great in a bow tie and loafers."

SEVEN

"We're here." Casey reached down and unzipped the screen on Dylan's collapsible crate. "Welcome to Catalina Island."

Dylan cut his snore short, popped both eyes open, and yawned. *A world-class snooze is the only way to start the day.*

Casey stood up on tiptoes and scanned the crowd. "Should we wait for Rita and Joe Friday?"

"Nah. Since we couldn't all sit together, Carl said to meet him on the dock at the golf cart station." Sumo grabbed his backpack.

Golf is a game with little, white balls. A cart carries stuff. Don't get it.

"Hold on, Little Buddy." Casey waited for the other passengers to pass. "You can come out now." He hooked Dylan's leash to his collar, led him out, and collapsed the crate.

"Give me Dylan's crate."

"Thanks." Casey handed it over and shrugged into his backpack. "Go ahead. We'll follow you."

They left the boat and walked down the dock. At the end of the dock Dylan stopped and did a one-eighty turn. *The water stretches out to the sky*. The sun beat down and kids walked by carrying surfboards. Music blared out from restaurants. Dylan studied the water and thought about his bath at Happy Paws. *This is a really big bathtub*.

At the golf cart station Carl waved his arm high in the air. "Over here, everybody."

Dempsey threw back his big head and howled. His four sturdy legs pounded saucer-shaped paws on the sand, kicking up a mini sandstorm.

"We're coming," Rita called from the boat. She slipped on her sunglasses and guided Joe Friday over to Carl. The big oaf jumped and danced on the end of his leash like a monkey on a string.

"Hard to believe Joe Friday will be on the Brea K-9 Unit," Sumo said.

Casey laughed. "He's goofy but he can run. The bad guys won't stand a chance." Casey picked Dylan up. "The sand is hot, Little Buddy. You can run around later."

Fine by me.

"We've got two golf carts," Carl said. "Rita you and Joe Friday, take that one." He led the way to the second golf cart. "Casey, Sumo and Dylan you can ride with us."

Sumo looked around. "We're missing somebody. You said four handlers and their dogs were coming."

Carl slapped an ugly beige hat on his head. "Change in plans. Just us."

Sumo and Casey tossed their backpacks in the storage space behind the cart. They piled into the back seat and Casey put Dylan between them. Dempsey hopped into the front seat.

Carl reached across Dempsey for the seatbelt and

clicked him into place. Carl turned around, "Seatbelts, guys."

"Come closer, Dylan." Casey stretched the belt across them both. "This is a bumpy ride."

Carl started the engine and the golf cart jerked to life. Dempsey gave an excited bark.

Casey rubbed Dylan's head. "This will be so much fun."

"Have you ever noticed," Sumo dug into his backpack for his baseball cap, "Catalina Island always looks the same."

Dylan jumped when three black birds raced the golf cart, wildly beating their wings. He leaned forward, getting a better look. His ears flapped in the wind and around his face. Dylan grinned happily. *Riding in a golf cart is almost like flying.*

They bumped along Clarissa Street and turned right on Tremont. "Our camp is coming up," shouted Carl over his shoulder. A few minutes later, he pulled into a dirt parking lot and turned off the ignition. "This is our base camp." He pointed to a large white pop-up tent. People in hats and sunglasses stood around drinking from water bottles. Labradors, Golden Retrievers, Great Danes, Boxers, and German Shepherds sat at their handlers' feet, tongues hanging out.

"Who are these people?" Sumo had his cell phone out and aiming it at the campsite.

"They're volunteers," Carl said. "Some I know from Search and Rescue. We have about ten other dogs here today. Some work Drug Enforcement." He undid his and Dempsey's seatbelts and got out. "Get your gear and follow me."

Dylan watched Casey grab his backpack from the

storage area. Dylan did a full circle on his seat. The water was gone, and he saw only hills, trees, and sky. Strange noises came from the trees and bushes. *Casey said Catalina is an island—whatever that is. It's not like home. What if I get lost?*

Casey lifted Dylan out and put him on the ground.

"Hi, Carl." A woman with an iPad and a black-and-white dog that came up to her waist stopped by the golf cart. "Let's get you checked in."

"Hi Marlo. Hi Rupert." Carl pulled some papers out of his pocket. "This is Casey, Sumo and Dylan." He gestured behind him. "You already know Rita and Joe Friday."

Marlo searched for something on her iPad. "Got it. Come over to the tent. We're about to discuss today's agenda." She pointed to dog bowls lined up outside the tent. "Make sure you water your dogs. There's bottled water for you in the cooler. Be sure you take plenty with you." She went back to her iPad. "We've marked the area into four grids, so we have four groups going out today. You and your friends will be one group. Carl, I have you as the field leader."

"Thanks."

Casey jiggled Dylan's leash. "Let's go."

Dylan pulled back. *All these dogs are tall.*

"Look," Casey crouched down, "today is all about having fun. Don't worry if the other dogs know more than you do. It's okay to be new. They were once new, too."

Whine.

"Remember, you're smart," he grinned, "and grumpy old Roger thinks you have potential."

Potential is good. Whatever that is.

"I'll make a deal with you. If there's time before we get on the boat tonight, I'll take you to the ice cream shop."

Okay!

They joined the others and stood around Marlo. She waited until she had their attention. "We're going to start with a game of hide-and-seek for about an hour. Field leaders, you can explain the rules. Then we'll go on to a search and rescue activity."

Carl took Casey, Sumo, Rita, and the dogs to a spot away from the others but near trees and bushes. He dug into his pocket and came out with two Ziploc treat bags. "Here."

Things are looking up.

"Hide-and-seek is fun," Carl began, "and that's what makes this so easy for the dogs to learn. Let me show you."

Carl extended both hands, showing his second and third fingers to Dempsey. "Watch."

Dempsey parked his rump on the ground and kept his eyes on Carl.

Carl trotted to a bush and hid behind it. "Find me, Dempsey. Find Carl."

Dempsey leaped up and arrowed in on Carl.

"Good boy, Dempsey." Carl rubbed his hands over the big dog's head. Dempsey shoulder-bumped Carl's thigh. "All right." Carl pulled a treat out of his Ziploc bag and Dempsey gulped it down.

"That doesn't seem too hard," Sumo said. "Dempsey saw you hide."

"All lessons start easy. It's important to build the dog's confidence. Rita, you try it."

Rita stepped in front of Joe Friday and waited.

"When you give him the hand signal for Watch, say Watch at the same time."

Joe Friday wasn't interested. He plopped down and started digging up dirt with his snout.

Rita flapped her hand in his direction and then gave the command. "Watch."

Joe Friday kept digging, making his little mound of dirt bigger.

Rita heaved out a sigh and tried the command again. "Joe Friday. Watch."

Joe Friday flipped over onto his back and wiggled in the dirt.

Rita's shoulders slumped and she looked to Carl.

"Touch him gently on his muzzle. When he looks at you, say Watch."

She tried it. Joe Friday heaved to his feet. He hitched up his right, back paw and scratched his stomach. Then he licked her hand.

"He's not getting it."

"Let him see you take a treat out of the bag. Slowly, bring it to his nose. When he looks at it say, Watch."

Rita did and Joe Friday gave her his full attention.

Carl stepped in and took Joe Friday's leash. "Go hide behind the bush and call him."

When Rita got to the bush she dropped out of sight. "Find me, Joe Friday. Find Rita."

Carl let go of the leash. Joe Friday rocketed into the air. He landed on all fours, whipped around, and started chasing his tail.

"Call him again."

Sumo leaned toward Casey. "K-9 Unit, really?"

The bad guys don't have a thing to worry about.

Carl picked up Joe Friday's leash. "Find Rita." Carl led him around the bush. When Rita popped her head up, Joe Friday leaped high and planted his big paws on her shoulders like they'd been apart for a year. "Give him the treat and praise him."

Rita did and Joe Friday slid to the ground.

Casey winked at Dylan. "You have this, Little Buddy."

Do you have a treat?

Casey stood in front of Dylan, dropped his leash, and said, "Watch", giving him the hand signal.

I'm watching for the treat.

Casey loped over to the bush and ducked down. "Find me, Dylan. Find Casey."

Dylan zipped over to the bush and whacked a paw on Casey's knee. *Treat time.*

"Good boy! Awesome!"

Sumo ran over to them, holding his cell phone in the air as he went. "Attention, Dylan's Dog Squad. While the world watches and waits, Dylan makes his first rescue on Catalina Island."

Casey pushed Sumo's cell phone aside but laughed. "Isn't that a bit much?"

Sumo made a face. "After Joe Friday? No way. That dog is dumb."

"Hey," Casey put a finger to his lips. "Don't make Rita feel bad. I was just telling Dylan it's okay to be new."

They went through the exercise a few more times. When Joe Friday finally got the hang of it, Carl called a water break.

Casey dug Dylan's collapsible water dish out of his backpack and filled it with water. "Whew! It's always so hot here in July." He found his Angels cap and put it on.

"Yeah." Sumo downed his water bottle.

Carl came over. "For our search and rescue today, we're going to take the golf carts up the road and behind the hill. The brush is dense." He gave Casey and Rita each a Ziploc bag. "Don't open them yet. We'll wait until we're there to give the dogs the scent."

Casey held the bag up. Inside there were ribbons and a tiny sleeve from a sweater. The same things were in Rita's bag. "We're looking for a kid?"

Rita eyebrows shot up. "Are you serious?"

"Hey, kids get lost all the time." Carl straightened his hat. "Something else you should know. It's been a very dry summer. Catalina Island has a problem with coyotes, like we do. We must be careful. At this time of the day, coyotes like to stay in the brush and keep cool. But if they're hungry, they'll venture out." He looked at Dylan. "A coyote will take anything under eighty pounds. Keep your dogs close."

Rita wasn't sure. "This is a search and rescue activity. What about when I let Joe Friday off leash to go find?"

"Joe Friday is big, but I suggest you keep him on leash." Carl pulled the brim of his cap down. "If you're not comfortable doing this, that's okay. What about you, Casey?"

I don't want to be a coyote treat.

"We're here for fun. Dylan's staying on the leash. Right, Little Buddy?"

Right, Buddy.

"Fair enough. Let's go."

Sumo, Casey, and Dylan got into the back seat again. Dylan scooted over and let Casey put the seat belt around them.

Carl started the golf cart and swung out of the parking lot. Dylan lifted his face up, catching the cool breeze. *Today is the best day.*

Suddenly something streaked across the road and Carl slammed on the breaks. "Sorry. The island has a lot of rabbits."

Dylan swiveled his head around, watching slim paws disappear into the scrub. *Rabbits are fun!*

"Catalina Island is kind of like a big Carbon Canyon Park." Casey pointed to something with a bushy tail scampering up a tree. "That's a squirrel." He lifted Dylan's head up. "Hawks just like the ones at home. There are foxes, mountain lions, rattlesnakes, and even wild pigs out here. All kinds of animals."

Which ones munch Cocker Spaniels?

Sumo grinned. "My favorite is still the bison."

Dylan pawed Casey's knee. *What's a bison?*

"Imagine Dempsey wearing a big furry rug on his head and shoulders."

Scary.

EIGHT

Carl eased the golf cart to a stop. "This is it."

Rita pulled alongside them. Joe Friday sat open-mouthed next to her, swinging his big head left and right, sending out sprays of doggie spit. Rita wiped the side of her cheek.

"We're on the other side of the island." Casey helped Dylan out and grabbed his backpack.

Sumo checked his cell phone. "Cell phone service sucks."

Carl jutted his chin to the clearing. "You'll be able to pick up a signal soon." He patted his belt. "I have my radio, just in case. Let's go set up."

Dylan trotted alongside Casey, the sun warming his shoulders. *What's that?* Dylan pounced toward a lizard doing pushups on a flat rock.

"That's a Southern Alligator Lizard," Casey said, pointing. "They can get to be seventeen inches long. Hey, Sumo, remember when one crawled in that kid's sleeping bag at camp? Man, that kid could scream."

Sumo punched him in the arm. "That was me, you idiot. I still hate those things."

Dylan tried to sniff the lizard, but the lizard sliced the air with its tail. *Never mind.*

"I'm going to keep you close, Dylan," Casey said, "but whatever you do, don't chase the skunks."

"Oh man." Sumo busted up. "Ms. D would go crazy if Dylan got skunked."

Dylan cocked his head. *What's a skunk?*

"Skunks look like striped cats."

What's a cat?

"Here are your maps," Carl said. "Our team has grid number two." He pointed to an area on the map. "I've divided it into three sections. I'll take this section here." He pointed again, "Rita, you're here. Casey and Sumo, you're over there. The direction is north. Check your compass app now and make sure it's working."

They did.

Carl handed Rita and Casey a bag of small flags. "Use a flag every time your dog alerts and finds something, like a piece of fabric or candy bar wrapper. Anything that could tell you the one you're tracking passed by. When you find something or your dog alerts, contact me. I'll call it in to Marlo at Base Camp."

"Who is lost?" Rita asked.

"Lily. She's four years old and probably scared."

Dylan sidled close to Casey. *I never want to be lost.*

"Remember to call Lily's name every few minutes. Remember to water your dog often. Remember to give him the scent often. Remember to give him lots of praise."

Remember to give me lots of treats.

Sumo squinted under his baseball cap. "When you and Dempsey go out, do you always find the person?"

"Sometimes we don't and that's hard to take." Carl huffed out a breath. "Luckily, this is only an activity. No matter what, we're out for two hours and then Marlo will signal us back to Base Camp. Ready?"

Rita, Casey, and Sumo nodded.

"Get the Ziploc bags out. The ones I gave you with Lily's belongings."

They did.

Carl brought his out and gave Dempsey the Watch command. Dempsey sat, watching Carl's face. Carl opened the Ziploc bag, took out a long purple ribbon, and brought it close to Dempsey's nose. "This is Lily. Dempsey, find Lily."

Dempsey got to his feet, raised his big head, and scented the air.

"Good dog," Carl praised. "Rita, you try it."

Sumo brought his cell phone out and held it up. "I've gotta get this."

Rita brought the sweater sleeve out of the bag and held it in front of Joe Friday's nose. "This is Lily. Joe Friday, find Lily."

Joe Friday sniffed it, and Rita beamed like a proud parent. Then Joe Friday lunged for the sleeve, clamped his jaws on it, and shook it.

"Hey!" Rita yelped, letting go.

Carl kept his grin to himself, but Sumo was laughing so hard he dropped his cell phone.

Casey picked Dylan up and buried his face in his ear, so Rita wouldn't see him laughing. "I hope we don't have to rescue them," Casey whispered.

No way. You promised me ice cream later.

"Try it again, Rita."

"Uh, okay." She brought out a hair ribbon. Using the tips of two fingers, she held the ribbon out at arm's length and dangled it in front of Joe Friday's nose. "This is Lily. Joe Friday, find Lily."

Grr, ruff! Joe Friday wagged his tail and rolled his big brown eyes. He shot out his tongue, snagged the ribbon and gulped it down.

"Oh man," Sumo crowed and brought his cell phone up to take a picture, "that ribbon is gone."

I don't want to know where it went.

"Carl," Rita wailed, "he's not catching on."

"He will. All dogs do. Usually. Maybe." Carl took her map from her and used a yellow highlighter. "Start walking with him here, go here and then circle around until you're back here. Stop frequently and let him smell something from the bag. Give him the command to find Lily each time. Okay?"

Rita nodded and Joe Friday sat down and scratched his ear.

"Casey, give Dylan the scent and the command to find."

Casey held his hands out, signed and said, "Watch."

Dylan watched.

Casey brought the sleeve of the sweater out and held it to Dylan's nose. "This is Lily. Dylan, find Lily."

Dylan sniffed. *I know this smell. Lily? Whine.*

"Good." Carl nodded. "He's got the scent. Let's head out. Remember, water the dogs often and check in with me often. No matter what, we're back here in two hours. Got that?"

"We're off!" Sumo announced.

Casey gave Dylan the scent again. "This is Lily. Dylan, find Lily."

Dylan shook his ears. *Lily?*

"This is kind of neat but kind of weird." Sumo shifted

his backpack and trudged along. "I know it's an activity but it's a lot of pressure."

Casey checked his compass app and motioned to his left. "Especially since a kid is lost."

They walked for about twenty minutes, calling Lily's name, until Dylan stopped by a bush. He sniffed around, plopped his buns down and whined. *Lily.*

"What is it, Dylan?" Casey got a flag out of the bag and stuck it in the ground. He searched around the bush. "I don't see anything."

Whine.

"What now?" asked Sumo.

Casey brought out his cell phone. "Carl, I think we're on the right track. Dylan stopped at a bush and whined."

"That's good. Footprints? Any bits of cloth? Blood?"

"The path is pretty messed up. There are lots of footprints."

"Keep me posted."

Casey gave Dylan a treat. "Good boy." He pulled Dylan's collapsible water dish from his backpack and filled it.

Dylan stuck his muzzle in the dish and lapped up the water. When he finished, he licked the bowl. *More?*

"I know. It's hot." Casey filled the dish again. "How are you doing, Sumo?"

He gave a thumbs up.

"Let's go." Casey brought the sweater sleeve out of the bag. "This is Lily. Dylan, find Lily."

"Lily," Sumo called. "Lily."

Dylan took off in the same direction. About fifteen minutes later, he alerted again. *Arf!*

This time he strained on the end of his leash, trying to circle a big rock. *Lily.*

Casey planted another flag and called Carl. "It's me again. Dylan alerted at a rock, but I don't see anything."

"His nose is better than yours. Keep me posted."

"Okay." Casey gave Dylan a treat and rubbed his back. "You're doing great. Want some water?"

Dylan didn't wait for Casey to finish filling the dish but stuck his tongue in. *Thirsty.*

Sumo sighed. "Carl must know where the kid is, right?"

"Yeah."

"I wish he'd tell us if we're getting close." Sumo turned his baseball cap around backwards. He dug into his backpack for his bandana and wiped his forehead. "I'd hate to be tromping around out here for nothing."

"Suck it up." Casey got his and Dylan's bandanas out, poured water on them, and used them to wipe their faces. He tied his around his neck and shoved Dylan's into his pocket.

"It's gotta be ninety-five out here."

Dylan licked his lips. Sumo was making some good points.

Casey looked at the map and then his compass app. "We need to go over there."

"Joe Friday! Help! Somebody help me!"

"Hey, that's Rita," Casey said, bringing Dylan closer to him. "Coyotes?"

Sumo already had his cell phone out. "Carl, something's happened. Rita's in trouble."

"Tell me where you're at. I'm coming."

Sumo rattled off the compass coordinates.

A blur of small black-and-white animals raced into the clearing, hissing, and puffing. Tiny feet stomped.

"Oh, no," Sumo whispered. "This isn't good."

Why? Dylan checked out the furry striped animals with the bushy tails. *They look friendly.*

"Skunks." Casey kept his eyes glued on them and slowly lowered himself until he was crouched beside Dylan. He put his arm around Dylan. "Stay still, Little Buddy."

Joe Friday shot into the clearing, kicking up dirt and dragging his leash. Happy to see Dylan, he bounded over and plopped down beside him.

Go away. You're in trouble. Dylan scooted closer to Casey. *You brought the skunks.*

Joe Friday was clueless. He wiggled his buns, threw his head back and howled.

"Quiet!" Casey and Sumo shouted.

That's all it took. The skunks whipped around, hunched their backs into horseshoes, lifted their tails, and released.

Whoa! Dylan's eyes watered. He shook his ears, dropped down, covered his nose with his front paws and wriggled in the dirt.

Casey jumped up, dropping Dylan's leash, and covering his eyes. "Holy, moly, joly!"

The smell didn't bother Joe Friday a bit, so he tipped his head back and howled again.

Agh! Dylan rolled onto his stomach, rubbed his eyes with both paws, and blinked up at Casey. *What is that smell?*

"Oh man," Casey and Sumo said together.

Sumo pulled his T-shirt up to cover his nose.

The skunks disappeared into a group of trees, but they didn't take the smell with them.

Behind Casey, Dylan and Sumo, the bushes parted, and Rita stumbled out, red-faced and gasping. She stopped, bent over at the waist, and gulped in air. "Get." She kept one hand on her knee, raised her head and flopped a limp hand in their direction.

"Joe Friday," Sumo filled in for her and starting walking toward the dog.

Rita nodded and panted, "He thinks skunks are fun."

No way. They're smelly.

"Man, those little guys stink." Casey reached down for Dylan's leash. "Let's get out of here, Little Buddy."

I'm ready. Dylan started walking but froze when Casey signed Stop.

Hissing, snorting sounds were coming from the bushes again.

Dylan craned his neck to see. *What's that?*

Skunks sprinted into the clearing. Black-and-white heads swung in Joe Friday's direction, but their paws didn't slow down.

Joe Friday didn't know sign language, but he knew the race was on. *Arf! Arf!* The big dog leaped up, doggie-grinned at Sumo, and galloped after the skunks.

"Joe Friday! No! Stay!" Rita shouted but he kept going. "Guys," she turned back to them, "you've got to help. He's going to get skunked." She wrung her hands, dropped her voice, and struggled for words, "You know Joe Friday is training for the Brea Police K-9 Unit."

Incredible.

"You may not believe this but," she went on.

Joe Friday's not smart?

"Sometimes he gets lost."

"Rita," Sumo cracked up, "Catalina is an island. How far can he go?"

"You're not helping," Casey muttered and brought out his cell phone. "Where's Carl? He should've been here by now." Casey found Carl's number on his cell phone and tried it. "That's weird. It went to voicemail."

"Guys, please help." Rita flung both her hands out wide. "Joe Friday could already be lost."

"We'll find him." Casey waggled Dylan's leash. "All we have to do is follow the smell."

Joe Friday's bark exploded from somewhere in the trees, punctuated by high pitch yips guaranteed to shatter glass.

"Get this mutt out of here!" A familiar voice bellowed. "No! No! For cryin' out loud!"

Rita hesitated. "Is that who I think it is?"

Casey, Dylan, and Sumo exchanged looks.

Oh yeah.

"Well," Casey tried hiding a grin, "the good news is Joe Friday isn't lost."

Sumo turned to Rita. "You should go first. Joe Friday could be hurt."

Rita considered this.

"And need your help," Casey prompted.

She took a few steps and stopped. "Are you coming?"

Do we have to?

"Who belongs to this dog?" the angry voice yelled. "Carl, I know you're out there. Is this idiot canine one of yours?"

"Oh, yeah," Casey agreed. "We're right behind you."

Way behind you.

Sumo had his cell phone out. "Social media is going to love this."

"This is the stupidest dog on the planet! Get him out of here."

"Wait a minute, Little Buddy." Casey got Dylan's bandana out of his pocket. He poured water on it, tied it around Dylan's neck and pulled it over his nose. "This will help."

Casey and Sumo pulled their bandanas up and over their noses. Casey started laughing. "I know this isn't funny."

"Oh, yeah, it is."

Dylan tried sucking in air and the bandana stuck to his snout. *No, it's not.*

Casey waved a hand in front of his face. "Man, this stinks."

They walked through the trees and into a clearing. The skunk smell was in full force.

Roger was walking in circles, eyes watering, yelling, and pointing at Rita. In the crook of his arm, he held a tiny white poodle, wide-eyed and shaking.

"I'm really sorry." Rita took a step toward Roger but changed her mind when her eyes started to water.

Joe Friday didn't mind a bit and was happily sniffing and barking at the bushes. When he came up empty, he shook his meaty head and trotted over to Rita, dropping his rump on the ground.

"Joe Friday's still a puppy, still in training."

"You're wasting your time and money, lady. Your dress size is higher than that mutt's IQ."

"Oh!" Rita burst into tears. "You're mean."

Dempsey galloped into the clearing, scented the air, skidded to a stop, and turned tail. Carl came out of the trees. "Hi, Roger."

"Don't 'Hi, Roger' me. Thanks to this mutt, Lily and I got skunked."

Casey and Sumo turned to each other and mouthed, "Lily?"

Lily?

"Get out!" Sumo busted up laughing. "We've been tracking a poodle?"

She looks like a woobie.

"Amazing," Casey whispered, "Roger has a little frou-frou dog."

Dylan leaned against Casey and looked up at him. *I'm taller than Lily.*

"I told you we'd have fun today, Little Buddy. We're definitely getting ice cream."

Dylan sighed happily. *Today was the best day. I'll never forget it.*

NINE

Dylan stretched out on his stomach and sniffed his front legs. *It's nice to be clean again, even if I had to get wet all over.* He hooked his two paws over the edge of Casey's bed and wiggled his butt. *I could get down, but the floor is hard. This is much better.* He rolled onto his side and snuffled the bedspread.

"Almost ready, Little Buddy," Casey called from his closet. "I can't find my flip-flops."

No surprise. Dylan waited for Casey to come out and start looking around the room. *We do this every day.*

Casey opened his backpack and rooted inside. "Nope." He tossed it onto a chair and put his hands on his hips. "Dylan?"

Okay. Dylan hopped off the bed and went to his water dish. He got the flip-flop resting on top of the dish and dropped it on Casey's bare foot.

"Hey, thanks." Casey frowned. "Where's the other one?"

Dylan tummy-crawled under Casey's bed, got the flip-flop and butt backed out.

"Awesome." Casey balanced on one foot and then the other, wiggling into them. "Let's tell Mom we're leaving."

Outside her office, Casey slowed. He extended his left hand, palm up and sharply brought his right hand down to his left hand at a right-angle giving Dylan the hand signal to stop. Dylan waited while Casey listened. "I think it's okay. I don't hear anything."

They walked in and Dylan went over to Mom's chair. He pawed at her leg. She hefted him up and sank her face into his curly ears.

"You smell so good." Mom turned him around. "I know you enjoyed Catalina Island, but you came back filthy."

I found Lily.

"We had a blast. Dylan did everything right. Roger said it usually takes a dog longer to learn to track somebody, but Dylan's a natural."

"Why did Carl make up that story about Lily being lost? Why not say you were really looking for Roger? It would've made your job easier."

Casey laughed. "Carl was afraid we wouldn't try so hard to find Roger. The guy's such a grump."

"It's hard to believe Lily is really Roger's dog." She shook her head. "Especially after all the mean things he said about Dylan."

He said I was short.

"Just one of life's little mysteries."

She tapped her computer screen. "I've been looking into search and rescue programs. In California, you have to be sixteen to volunteer."

How old is that in dog years?

"That sucks."

She gave him The Look but let it go. "You'd have to learn first aid if you're serious about this. The Brea Community Center offers a class in the fall." She shrugged. "Dreams don't work unless you do."

"John Maxwell?"

Mom smiled. "For someone who doesn't like to read, you remember quotes."

Casey rubbed Dylan between the ears. "You give me no choice."

She smiled bigger. "What are you two doing today?"

"We're meeting Sumo at Brea's Ice Cream. Then we're going to his house to hang out."

Ice cream? Dylan squirmed and got down. *Let's go!*

"Only one scoop of ice cream for you, Casey. It's packed with sugar and fat. Dylan can have half a scoop of vanilla ice cream. Too much fat isn't good for him, either."

Dylan licked his lips. *Yes, it is.*

"Got it. What are you doing today?"

Mom huffed out a breath. "*Hieronymus the Hamster Goes to Nasa* has a book launch in a few days. I've got to contact Amazon, work on publicity—the usual." She pulled a stack of papers closer. "I need to get with Teri about *Hieronymus the Hamster Goes to South Korea.* She's started writing the story but I'm thinking," she added, trying to sound casual, "Teri should somehow include Dylan in the story. After all, he's from South Korea."

Dylan clamped his mouth shut. *I don't want to be in a story with that dumb hamster.*

Casey rolled his eyes. "Let me guess. This way you can get some 'excellent publicity' for Cranky Pants's book."

"Well," she tossed it aside, "it wouldn't hurt."

"I don't get why Dylan has to share the spotlight with Hieronymus."

You tell her, Casey.

"Hmm." Her eyes slid to Dylan. "You might have given me an idea."

Casey tugged on Dylan's leash. "Let's get out of here before she thinks of something else."

They found Sumo already at Brea's Ice Cream. He was collapsed on a chair at an outside table with his skinny legs stretched out in front of him. "Hey."

Casey got Dylan's blanket out of his backpack and spread it on the ground. "Unless you want another bath, stay on this."

Dylan turned two circles, kicked the blanket into a pile with his back paws, and plopped down. *Okay.*

"It's so hot. Great day for ice cream." Sumo stood up. "I'm having pistachio. What do you want? I'll get it."

Casey gave him a ten-dollar bill. "Mocha fudge in a cup. Dylan will have vanilla in a junior cup."

Sumo picked up the money. "Back in a minute."

Dylan watched Sumo disappear inside Brea's Ice Cream. Through the window he could see employees serving ice cream to people in line. *It would be awesome to have a job that lets you eat ice cream all day.*

Sumo came back carrying three dishes of ice cream and set them on the table. He took his and dug in.

Dylan popped up, put his front paws and muzzle on the table. *I'm ready.*

"Hold on." Casey spooned half of Dylan's vanilla ice cream onto his.

That's mine!

"Mom would kill me if you got sick."

I won't tell.

Casey put the cup of ice cream on the blanket and Dylan dropped down. "Hold on."

Now what?

Casey held Dylan's ears away from his face. "Now you can dig in."

"I've never seen a dog that liked ice cream so much." Sumo scraped the last of his and licked the spoon.

"I don't think he ever had ice cream until he came to America."

"July is like National Ice Cream Month or something." Sumo waved the spoon in the air. "I think it has its own day."

"No kidding."

No kidding. Dylan licked a little ice cream off his nose. *That's a very good day.*

Sumo wiped his lips with the back of his hand. "There's a cardboard cutout thing inside the store that says, 'Win Free Ice Cream Contest.'"

Casey pushed his empty cup away. "Are you talking about the kind of cardboard thing where you stick your face in a cutout, and someone takes your picture?"

"Yeah."

They both looked at Dylan.

"Want to check it out, Little Buddy?"

Burp.

Casey picked Dylan up and Sumo threw away their trash. When they went inside, everyone turned to look at them.

"Aw." "He's so cute." "Look at those ears." "Aw." "Look at those paws."

Dylan zeroed in on the ice cream in two long display cases. *Wow. That's a lot of ice cream. This place is even better than I thought.*

Casey and Dylan went behind the cardboard cutout. "Okay, when you put your face in here," Casey put his face in the oval opening and brought it out again, "Sumo will take your picture."

Casey tried leaning Dylan forward. Dylan put out both paws and pushed away from the cardboard cutout.

"Don't worry. I've got you." Casey put his face in again and brought it out. "See?"

"Ready?" Sumo held his cell phone up.

"Yeah, here we go." Casey leaned Dylan forward and Dylan put his face in the oval opening.

"Got it."

They came around and waited while Sumo checked his cell phone.

"Great photo but I need to get rid of some of the background." He tapped a few times and sent it out to social media. "Wait until Dylan's Dog Squad sees this."

"Did you see that?" Casey pointed to the writing on the cardboard cutout sign.

Sumo read out loud. "'Win Free Ice Cream Contest. Email us your best story about ice cream. If chosen, your story will appear on our website. You will receive two gallons of our delicious ice cream every month for one year'."

"Wow," Casey and Sumo said together.

Wow.

"What's the catch?" Casey asked.

Sumo looked closer. "No catch but today's the last day to email a story."

"What do you think?"

Dylan stretched up on hindlegs and pawed Casey. *Think faster.*

"We could do this," Casey said. "You know. Write something."

Now we're getting somewhere.

Sumo hooked a thumb over his shoulder. "We can write the email while we're here and send it to them."

They settled themselves at the outside table again.

"I've got the email open." Sumo waited. "What do you want to say?"

"What if we tell them about Dylan's life? We—meaning you because I don't like to write—can say he's from South Korea. You can say my brother Aiden sent him to me because Dylan destroyed his apartment."

It's not a good idea to start with bad things first.

"After Dylan got here, he started learning sign language, graduated from Agility class, works in the Read to Me Program, works at Children's Hospital, and is going to have his own book series."

I have a lot of jobs.

Sumo's thumbs were tap dancing like crazy. "When do we get to the ice cream part?"

Yeah.

"Then you could say Dylan had his first search and rescue class on Catalina Island yesterday. Because of his great nose," Casey reached down and patted Dylan on his head, "he found Lily."

Sumo stopped typing. "Let's say four-year-old Lily. People are suckers for lost kids."

Lily is a poodle. Whine.

"Hmm." Casey patted Dylan again. "Should we say Lily is a dog?"

Casey and Sumo thought about that for a second. "Nah."

Casey leaned forward. "Here's the big finish. Because Dylan saved the day, he got to have ice cream. You can say he loves vanilla ice cream more than anything."

"Got it." Sumo read it to himself and pressed send.

Casey rubbed his stomach. "I'm still hungry."

"Me, too."

Me, three.

"Mom would freak out if I got another ice cream." Casey looked at the Brea's Ice Cream sign. "She didn't say anything about a milkshake. Want one?"

Yes! What's a milkshake?

Sumo was studying his screen on his cell phone. "Yeah. Chocolate." He paused long enough to dig out some money. He looked over his shoulder at the store. "You'd better hurry up. It's starting to get crowded."

"Okay." Casey tied Dylan's leash to his chair. "Be right back, Little Buddy."

Arf! Dylan collapsed onto his blanket.

"Hey, Dylan." "Hi." "Thanks for the ice cream tip."

Dylan swiveled his head at the attention. *Arf!* He sat up straight when friendly hands reached down and petted him. *People are nice. I like having friends.*

"Check this out, Dylan." Sumo pointed to the stream of cars coming into the parking lot and taking the first parking space they came to. People jumped out and headed to Brea's Ice Cream like they were being chased. "Everybody wants ice cream."

Whine. I hope they don't eat it all before we get ours.

"Casey is taking forever," Sumo grumbled, getting up. He stood on tiptoes to look in the store window. "Oh, okay. He's paying for our milkshakes now."

Whew.

Casey came out and put the milkshakes on the table. "It's like a mob in there. They all arrived at once." He took Dylan's collapsible dish out of his backpack and poured some of his vanilla milkshake into it.

Dylan sniffed it and looked up at Casey. *Smells like ice cream.*

"I know what you're thinking but you're wrong. Mom said only one scoop of ice cream for me and half a scoop for you."

Uh-huh.

"We can have this because ice cream is frozen. A milkshake is like melted ice cream, totally different. Try it."

Dylan stuck his tongue in it. *Like it!*

Sumo unwrapped a paper straw, stuck it into the milkshake and stirred it. "Did you see the parking lot?"

A car and a truck were stopped side-by-side, the drivers arguing over the last parking space.

Casey shrugged. "People get weird in hot weather. What do you think of the milkshake, Little Buddy?"

Dylan polished it off. *Yes!*

Casey took a napkin and wiped Dylan's face. "Getting rid of the evidence."

Sumo sucked up the last of his milkshake. "Isn't that Sergeant Yelin getting out of the cruiser?"

Oh no. Dylan watched him go into the ice cream shop. *Are bad guys stealing the ice cream?*

"Maybe somebody had a heart attack or something."

Sumo shook his head. "Nah. They'd be an emergency vehicle here."

Dylan sighed happily. *Nothing to worry about.*

TEN

"What's the big deal, Mom?"

"You started a stampede on ice cream." She straightened her summer dress and tried to get comfortable in the hard wooden chair. "We're at the police station for the second time in a week. Brea's Ice Cream had to close early because they couldn't control the crowd."

"You'd think they'd be happy for the business," Sumo said.

She slid her eyes to him. "Do not speak."

Dylan kept his whine to himself.

"Why can't Brea Police Department spring for comfortable chairs?" Casey grumbled. "These are like sitting on rocks." Casey lifted Dylan up and put his blanket on the chair under him. "Try this."

Dylan shifted on his paws and almost slipped off. *Yikes.*

The office door swung open. Captain Rizzoli came in, went around her desk and sat down. She picked up a pen and pointed it at Casey and Sumo. "Start talking."

Casey gave her his best grin. "You're going to think this is funny."

"Doubtful."

"Brea's Ice Cream had this cardboard cutout in the store. You know the kind where you stick your face in and take a picture? Since it was their idea, we never would've thought of it on our own, we took Dylan's picture and put it on social media."

"Yeah," Sumo jumped in. "Then we were outside, just minding our own business. Everyone started showing up and going crazy. You'd think they'd never had ice cream on a hot day before."

Captain Rizzoli slid over a picture of Dylan framed in the oval cutout and pointed above his face. "This says, 'Free Ice Cream'."

Casey and Sumo exchanged looks.

Oh-oh.

"Yeah, well," Sumo said, "I guess a tiny, tiny bit of 'Win Free Ice Cream Contest' got cut off when I took the picture."

Captain Rizzoli tapped her pen on the desk. "Colleen?"

"It was an innocent mistake."

Captain Rizzoli frowned. She didn't see it that way. "Who wrote the email?"

Sumo and Casey pointed to each other.

Captain Rizzoli's frown deepened. "Dylan?"

I can't write.

She tossed her pen onto the desk and sighed. "I've been talking to Brea's Ice Cream for the last hour," she paused, "or rather they've been talking to me." She sat back in her chair. "Here's the thing. You caused a big mess for them. A lot of people came to the store expecting to get free ice cream and didn't."

"We're sorry." Casey took Dylan's face in his hands and turned it toward her. "You know how cute Dylan is.

He took a really cute picture. We wanted to enter their contest because Dylan likes their vanilla ice cream so much."

It's yummy.

Captain Rizzoli rolled her eyes. "That's the rub. Your social media blast shut them down today, but it also brought them a lot of attention. Their corporate office wants to take advantage of it. They liked the email you wrote about Dylan and asked me if it was true. I said he's a great dog and has accomplished a lot in a short time. They were so impressed they want to put Dylan's email on their website to promote their ice cream."

Will they give me ice cream?

Mom clapped her hands together. "That's really exciting."

Casey snickered. "You're thinking about free publicity for your books."

She gave a pretty smile. "We can both benefit from today."

Captain Rizzoli agreed. "I told the corporate office no one does publicity like Colleen Donovan. It was amazing how much money you raised for our Animal Shelter."

"Thank you." Mom brightened. "My pleasure."

"I told them about your company and that you have new books lined up for release. In fact, a book launch for *Hieronymus the Hamster Goes to Nasa* is scheduled for the Brea Country Club, correct?"

"Yes," Mom hesitated. "It's a barbecue event with live music and dancing."

"Excellent. When I told Brea's Ice Cream my idea, they agreed to work with you."

"What idea," Mom came forward in her chair. "Work with me in what way?"

"At your book launch, you'll provide an ice cream station, featuring Brea's Ice Cream with all the fixings."

"Okay," she dragged it out. "What else?"

Dylan licked his lips and pawed Casey's arm. *I want to go to Mom's book launch. What's an ice cream station with all the fixings?*

"Casey and Sumo will donate their time by assisting the staff of Brea's Ice Cream."

"Fine." Mom brought out her cell phone and started taking notes. "I'll get right on this."

"Maybe my mom won't let me," Sumo argued.

Mom froze him with a look. "I'll fix it."

"The very best part, in their opinion, is Dylan will be there for photo ops." Captain Rizzoli picked up the photo of Dylan and studied it. "Honestly, Dylan, I don't think you can take a bad picture."

I get to go! Yay!

Mom was coming around. "I'll ask Jonah to cover the story. Maybe get Anna or Sasha to do the photos." She tapped something on her cell phone. "I can get a blast out tonight." She smiled. "Great ideas. I like them."

Casey slid down in his chair. "You didn't ask us."

"No," Captain Rizzoli and Mom said together.

ELEVEN

Mom, Casey, and Dylan entered the Brea Library and walked to the receptionist's desk. The place was crowded. Kids and parents were everywhere.

"Hi, Lydia."

"Good afternoon." Lydia D'Angelo came around her desk and knelt to pet Dylan. "Hi, Handsome."

Dylan pranced in place. *I'm wearing my Read to Me bandana.*

"Casey and Dylan are a few minutes early for the Read to Me Program," Mom told her. "I hope that's okay. I have an appointment with Robert to discuss *Hieronymus the Hamster Goes to Nasa.*"

"Of course." Lydia beamed. "Thank you so much for sending us tickets to the book launch at the Brea Country Club. We're thrilled."

"You'll be pleased to know Dylan will be doing photo ops at the book launch."

"Really." Lydia ran her hands over Dylan's ears. "Count me in."

Two little girls hurried past them, carrying books, and heading for the Young Readers section.

"I'm reading first."

"No, you're not!"

Mom looked at the crowd in the Young Readers section. "You have a full house today. Is there anything Casey and Dylan should know?"

"Yes." Lydia motioned them to follow her. "Do you see the little boy in the dinosaur T-shirt? His name is Luca and he's six years old. He and his parents were in a terrible accident about a month ago. Both parents died. Luca is living with his grandmother now."

That's sad.

"He's in a new school. His grandmother says he's having trouble learning, he hasn't made any friends, and he hasn't spoken since the accident."

"If he doesn't talk," Casey asked, "how is he going to read?"

Lydia smiled. "His grandmother is hoping he might enjoy being with Dylan today. Luca can look at the pictures and you can read what's on the page."

Dylan looked up at Casey. *Now you'll have to stick around. You won't be able to take off like you usually do.*

"Okay."

Dylan liked the Young Readers section. Casey said it had a jungle theme—whatever that was. The walls were painted with the funny faces of tigers, elephants and giraffes peeking over low bookcases. Three stuffed penguins were marching around a giant igloo and a big bird with long feathers sat in an enormous tree. When kids walked by, it made a strange sound. Brightly colored beanbag chairs littered the floor. Kids were already lined up with their books at a long, green couch swirled like a goofy snake in front of the windows. *They're waiting for me!*

Mom checked her cell phone for the time. "I'll be back after my meeting."

Casey waved her and Lydia off. "Ready, Dylan?"

Dylan hopped onto the couch and settled himself in the middle. *I hope somebody reads a story about dogs today.*

A little girl in long braids climbed onto the couch. She gave her book to Dylan.

I can't read.

Casey reached over Dylan and opened the book to the first page. "I remember this story. It's about a lion."

What's a lion?

She put a bookmarker under the first line. "Dande." She frowned. "Dande." She pointed to the letters. "D-a-n-d-e-l-i-o-n."

Casey leaned over. "Dandelion."

"Thanks. Dandelion lived in a desert," she began. "He wanted to go to the city."

Dylan looked at the picture. Dandelion was like a big dog with a shaved backside and a bush on his head. Dandelion had a long skinny tail, with hair on the end and huge teeth. *He must have a very big toothbrush.*

A boy was next with a book about balloons.

"That's it," Casey asked, flipping through the book. "Just balloons? How much can you say about a balloon?"

The kid yanked it back. "Plenty, buster. Listen and learn."

You're rude. Dylan learned balloons went up in the air. Balloons came down in the air. Sometimes people made animals out of balloons. *That's creepy.*

A girl wearing a T-shirt with an airplane on it slid a

book under his muzzle. "I'm going to be a pilot when I grow up. Have you ever been on an airplane?"

"Dylan came to America from South Korea on an airplane."

"Wow!"

I was in a dark, hot cargo hold for the whole trip. My water bottle came loose, and I was thirsty. Dylan whined. *Thanks for reminding me, Casey.*

She flipped open the book and it scraped Dylan's chin. "This is about Amelia Earhart. Like a hundred years ago, she was the first girl pilot to fly across the Atlantic Ocean."

What's the Atlantic Ocean?

"She did it all by herself."

Big deal. I flew from South Korea all by myself.

"Get outta here," Casey said when the next kid sat down. "I remember you from the last time."

Jerome smirked. "Same here, hot shot." He dragged a book the size of a coffee table onto his lap. "My mom's getting her hair done. I'm stuck here until she gets back, so don't give me any grief."

"What is it this time?" Casey snickered. "Some dopey book on stuff only geeks care about?"

"Ha! Like you'd know the difference." Jerome pointed to the title. "I got something simple for your pea-sized brain to understand—wormholes."

Dylan looked at the dark cover with swirly white stuff and dots. *Worms are wiggly things in the garden.*

"It's a speculative structure linking disparate points in spacetime and is based on a special solution of the Einstein field equations." Jerome cracked the book open. "Let us begin."

Dylan drifted off before Jerome finished the first page.

Dylan came to when the kid slid off the couch and tossed the book onto the floor.

"There's my mom."

"About time," Casey muttered and looked around. "Who's next?"

Luca. Dylan pawed Casey's arm. *He's waiting.*

"Hey," Casey motioned to Luca, "your turn."

Luca came over but stopped in front of them, gripping a small book.

I hope you picked a happy story.

Casey pointed to Luca's T-shirt. "Do you like dinosaurs?"

Luca nodded.

"Me, too." Casey moved down a bit so Luca could squeeze in. "I'm Casey. This is Dylan. Is your book about dinosaurs?"

Luca shook his head no and sat down. He gave the book to Casey and placed one hand on Dylan's shoulders. In his other hand he held a small red truck.

Dylan licked the boy's bare knee.

The boy smiled and put the truck beside him on the couch.

Casey looked at the book's cover. "Trucks? Dylan would like to know about trucks. Can I help you read to him?"

Luca waited while Casey opened the book to the first page.

"These are pretty cool," Casey said, pointing to the pictures. "I like the ones with the custom paint jobs."

Luca turned the pages while Casey read but he didn't say anything.

Dylan studied a picture of a truck hurtling off a mountain, into blue sky. Flames were painted on its side. *Is it on fire?* He looked at another one with two big round things on top of the truck cab. *Ears?*

When Casey finished reading, he closed the book. "Dylan and I will be here next week. Are you coming back?"

Luca nodded and left.

"That is one lonely kid." Casey sighed.

I hope he gets happy soon.

"I think that's it." Casey waited. When no one else came over he said, "Want to go find Mom?"

Yes! Dylan hopped off the couch and something fell on the ground. *Arf!*

"Oh, man." Casey picked up the toy. "Luca forgot his truck." He scanned the faces of the kids. "I don't see him. Maybe Ms. D'Angelo can make an announcement or something."

When they got to the receptionist's desk, they found a small woman with white hair talking very fast to Ms. D'Angelo. She was holding a blue backpack.

"He's gone. I've looked everywhere," the woman's voice cracked. "No one's seen him."

Ms. D'Angelo put her hands out, trying to calm the woman. When she saw Casey and Dylan, relief shot across her face. "Oh good. Casey, Dylan. This is Mrs. Renfro. She's Luca's grandmother. Have you seen him?"

"Yeah, he brought a book over," Casey waved behind him to the Young Readers section, "but he forgot this." Casey held the little red truck out to the grandmother.

Mrs. Renfro gasped. "That's Luca's! He takes it with him everywhere." She closed her eyes. "Luca was riding with his parents in their red truck when they were in the accident. He saw both parents die."

Dylan's ears flicked. *No wonder Luca is so sad.*

"He's probably looking for his truck." Ms. D'Angelo forced a cheery smile on her face. "Let me make an announcement." She pressed the intercom button on her desk phone. "Your attention, please. Will Luca Renfro please come to the receptionist's desk?"

They waited but Luca didn't come.

TWELVE

Rory came through the library doors with two other officers and went to the receptionist's desk. "Hi Lydia. We came as soon as you called."

"Mrs. Renfro, this is Lieutenant Kellan. He'll help you find Luca."

"We'll do everything we can, ma'am." Rory's voice softened. "Has Luca ever gone missing before? Not come home when he was supposed to?"

"No, no." Mrs. Renfro covered her face with her hands. Her body shook with sobs. "I'm sorry. My grandson has been through so much lately." She dropped her hands and squared her shoulders. "He and his parents were in an accident last month. They were killed. Luca is taking it hard." She swiped at her tears. "We all are."

Lydia handed Mrs. Renfro a tissue from the box on her desk. "Lieutenant Kellan, Luca doesn't know his way around. He hasn't made friends, yet."

"Have you tried calling his name? Sometimes the easiest way is the best."

"He won't answer." Mrs. Renfro sniffled into the tissue. "Luca hasn't spoken a word since the accident."

"Okay. What was he wearing, do you remember?"

She nodded. "A dinosaur T-shirt and shorts. Luca is six years old and small for his age." Mrs. Renfro brushed a hand across her forehead and managed a smile. "He has shaggy brown hair. We keep meaning to get it cut."

"Do you have a recent picture of him that you can send to me?"

"Yes." Mrs. Renfro searched through her cell phone and handed it over. "This one was taken a week ago."

Rory took the cell phone from her. He tapped a few keys, waited, and tapped some more. "I've sent out his picture." He handed the cell phone back to her. "This is a big help."

She put her cell phone away. "Thank you."

Rory nodded to the officers, and they took off in separate directions. "Please wait here. I'll be right back."

He went over to Mom, kissed her on the cheek and then nodded to Casey. "Hi, Sis." Bending down he brushed Dylan's topknot out of his eyes. "How'd it go today? Did you work hard?"

I like working. The Read to Me Program is an important job.

"Can you find Luca?" Mom asked. "His grandmother must be frantic."

"She's holding it together." He hooked a thumb over his shoulder. "She gave us a current picture of Luca and a description. The officers are questioning the people in the library now. I've dispatched every available unit."

Whine.

"Casey, when did you see Luca today?"

"He was the last kid. After he left, I noticed he'd

dropped his truck on the ground. We went to Ms. D'Angelo's desk so she could make an announcement over the loudspeaker. She told us he was missing."

"Did you notice anything unusual? Did Luca talk about anything?"

Casey shrugged. "He didn't talk at all. He brought a book over and we looked at it together. Right, Dylan?"

Arf! Tell him Luca was sad.

"This is a pretty big place." Mom shook her head. "Across the street is the Brea Mall, the parking structure and restaurants."

Rory nodded. "It's amazing how fast kids can move. Lydia says he doesn't know the area. That can be worse. If he was going somewhere, we might be able to figure it out, but if he's wandering around." Rory let it trail off.

Some chatter came from Rory's radio, and he walked away from them. When he came back, he wasn't smiling.

"That was my K-9 Unit. They're in Santa Ana for training. I've ordered them back, but in this traffic, it'll be at least forty-five minutes before they get here."

"That's too long, Uncle Rory."

"We have no choice but to wait. The Sheriffs wouldn't get here any faster with their Bloodhounds."

Dylan got on his hind legs and reached up for Casey. *What about me?*

"Not now, Little Buddy."

I'm not telling you I'm hungry, for once. Dylan's stomach rumbled. *Well, now I am.*

Mom put her purse over her shoulder. "We should go home and let you do your job."

"Mom, we can't just leave."

Exactly, Casey.

Rory put his hands on his gun belt. "Your mom is right. There's nothing you can do."

Arf! Arf!

"Okay, okay. We're going, Little Buddy. Hold on."

Dylan leaped up on his hind legs and grabbed Casey's backpack.

"Hey!" The backpack slid off Casey's shoulder and dropped to the ground. Dylan pounced on it. "Do you want me to give you a treat?"

Dylan whined. *I'm trying to give you an idea.* He pawed the backpack and raced over to Mrs. Renfro.

"Oh my!" the older woman said when Dylan planted himself at her feet.

Dylan got on his hindlegs and grabbed Luca's backpack from her. The woman screamed.

"Dylan!" Casey raced up. "I'm sorry, Mrs. Renfro. Dylan is still in training."

Dylan plopped down on his rump and stared at him.

The idea dawned slowly. "That's it." Casey picked up the backpack. "Do you have anything of Luca's in here? A shirt or socks? Anything he's worn lately?"

Mom and Rory joined them.

"What is it?" Rory asked.

Casey's words tumbled out. "Dylan can track Luca."

Arf! Now you're catching on.

Rory crossed his arms over his chest. "Casey, Dylan isn't trained in search and rescue."

Mom agreed. "We're talking about a missing child. Be reasonable."

"What have you got to lose? The K-9 Unit can't get here for forty-five minutes. Luca could be anywhere by then. Roger says Dylan has a great nose. Dylan found Lily on Catalina Island when no one else could."

Mom held up her index finger. "He's had one lesson, Casey."

"Mom!"

Mom!

Mrs. Renfro opened Luca's backpack and pulled out a sweatshirt. "What about this?"

Dylan waved his paws in the air. *Let me try.*

Rory's radio squawked and he walked away, clicking it on as he went. When he came back, he puffed out his cheeks. "Luca is not in the library and he's not in the court-yard outside. My officers have talked to people, but no one's seen him."

Mrs. Renfro's lower lip trembled. "You've got to find him. He's a little boy. He's," her eyes welled up with tears, "all I have."

Dylan pawed her leg. *You have us.*

"Okay, Casey," Rory said and looked around. "I can't tell you not to try but I can tell you not to interfere. When the K-9 Unit gets here, we need to do our job." He thought for a moment. "If you want to give Dylan the scent, fine."

Casey took the sweatshirt from Mrs. Renfro. "This is Luca. Dylan, find Luca."

Dylan sniffed the sweatshirt. *Arf!* Dylan scented the air and wiggled his butt.

Casey took the backpack from Mrs. Renfro and put the sweatshirt inside. "Uncle Rory, I'll check in with you every fifteen minutes." He tugged on the leash. "Let's go, Little Buddy."

Casey and Dylan went outside.

Dylan looked around and scented the air. He took a few steps toward the drinking fountain but stopped and turned around. *Luca wasn't here.*

Casey let him work his way across the courtyard. Dylan

sniffed at the door to the art gallery but kept going. He stopped at the stairs leading to the street.

Casey pulled Luca's sweatshirt out again and let him smell it. "This is Luca. Dylan, find Luca."

Arf!

"Luca!" Casey called. "Dylan is looking for you."

Dylan scented the air again and then sniffed along the ground. *Yes.* Dylan took the stairs one at a time, stopping to sniff each one. *Luca.* He continued down until he reached the sidewalk and greenbelt that ran along the street. Cars zipped past them, blowing back his ears.

Casey pulled Dylan close to him. "Never cross a street. Always stay on the sidewalk. Cars can't see you."

That's good to know. Does Luca know that?

Casey thought out loud, "A little kid isn't going to cross a busy street, if he doesn't have to. The mall is way over on the other side of the parking lot." Casey crouched down to the size of a six-year-old. "He wouldn't be able to see it."

Dylan stuck his nose in the grass. *Luca's been here.* Dylan kept his nose to the ground, his buns in the air, walking back and forth.

"Luca!" Casey called. "Dylan found your truck."

Casey waited and then tugged on Dylan's leash. "There's nothing over that way. Just the parking structure." He brought out his cell phone, tapped the screen, and brought it to his ear. "Uncle Rory, nothing yet." He listened. "Okay."

After Casey hung up, he did a slow circle. This time he sniffed the air. "I smell hamburgers and French fries. Red Robin isn't too far away. A little kid would know those smells." He checked the time on his cell phone. "He's probably getting hungry."

Me, too.

"This way."

Dylan pulled back, almost slipping out of his chain collar. *No. Luca smells are this way.*

"Careful." Casey adjusted Dylan's collar, back over his ears. "If you lose your collar, you could get lost, too."

I have a microchip. I'll never be lost. Dylan wiggled his ears. *Maybe kids should be microchipped.*

Casey ran a hand through his hair. "Carl said your nose was better than mine. Okay, Little Buddy, we'll check your way first. We can always come back."

Arf!

Dylan led the way down the sidewalk. Every few feet he stopped and sniffed or scented the air.

"Uncle Rory? Dylan is taking me to the parking structure," Casey said into his cell phone. "Yeah, I'll call, if there's anything." He put his cell phone in his pocket. "Luca! Dylan is looking for you."

Dylan picked up the pace. When he entered the parking structure, he raised his snout. *Arf! Arf!*

"Got something? I don't see anything."

Casey eyed the rows of cars. "This place is packed. We could be hunting all day. Luca! Luca!"

Dylan walked slowly down a row of cars, but he didn't stop at any one of them. *I know where Luca went!* He turned a corner and started up the second level.

Casey got his cell phone out again. "Uncle Rory, can you come to the parking structure? We're on the second level. Dylan is excited." Casey listened. "Okay."

Dylan leaped forward, pulling Casey on the end of his leash. His paws ate up the concrete, running as fast as he could. *We're coming!* Dylan saw Luca first. *Arf! Arf!*

Casey let Dylan's leash go and Dylan ran over to the boy.

Luca was sitting near the rear tire of a red truck. Dylan pounced on him, knocking him over, and slurping dog kisses on his face.

Luca laughed and put his arms around Dylan. Dylan kept the kisses coming.

"Hey," Casey said when he caught up. "Dylan's been looking for you."

Dylan sat down and Luca wiped Dylan slobber off his face.

A cruiser pulled up and Rory got out, talking into his radio. He helped Mrs. Renfro out of the backseat. Mrs. Renfro broke away and ran to Luca. "Luca! You scared me."

Casey and Dylan stepped away and stood by Rory.

"Amazing," Rory said. "How on earth did you think of this place?"

"I didn't. I wanted to go the other way, but Dylan tracked Luca here."

"Dylan, I owe you an apology." Rory gave him a mock salute. "Good job!"

Dylan's chest puffed with pride. *I like having a job.*

Mrs. Renfro guided Luca over to them. "Luca, has something to say."

"I'm sorry." He looked down at his feet. "I just wanted to find Mommy and Daddy's red truck."

THIRTEEN

"This is awesome," Sumo grabbed a slice of pizza from the box, kicked back on the couch, and put his feet up on the coffee table. He brought the slice up to his mouth, took a big bite and half the toppings slid off and onto his paper plate. "Your mom is so cool to get us peperoni pizza."

What's peperoni?

"You got peperoni pizza." Casey put his feet up on the coffee table and examined his slice. "I got veggies with organic marinara sauce on a thin wheat crust. I had to argue for low fat mozzarella cheese." He took a bite. "This is like eating school cafeteria food."

Dylan stretched out between Casey and Sumo. Dylan liked Sumo because he was a slob, ate a ton of food, and didn't mind sharing. Dylan swiped the peperoni slices and gooey cheese from Sumo's plate and gulped them down. *Hmm. Peperoni are spicy.* He checked out Casey's plate. *Not so interesting.* It was littered with something like cracker crumbs smeared with something red. His long tongue snagged them anyway. *Very dry.* Casey had picked off some spiky things he called broccoli from his pizza and had tossed them onto the plate. Dylan licked them and they stuck to his tongue. He spit them out and they fell on the floor.

"Sorry, Little Buddy. I should've warned you," Casey said. He reached for a piece of Sumo's pizza and peeled off the peperoni slices. He tossed them back into the box and offered some crust with marinara sauce to Dylan. "Here's what I'm missing."

Dylan sniffed and then took it with his front teeth. *That's more like it.*

"The *Back to the Future* movie marathon has already started." Sumo reached for the remote and geared up the TV. The movie flashed across the big screen. "These old movies are funny. All the stuff they thought was so cool back then, we have today."

"Check that out." Casey pointed to the clock tower in the movie. "Only old people use a clock or a watch. Everybody else uses a cell phone to tell time."

I use my stomach to tell me it's chow time.

"Well?" Mom walked in and stood in front of the TV, blocking the middle of the screen. She smiled, waited, and held her arms out and hands up like a W.

Casey stared. "What?"

Dylan stopped chewing.

Sumo held his half-eaten pizza slice in midair. "Uh."

She smoothed her long dress and stood up straight. "Well," she repeated.

Dylan swallowed and studied Mom. *Give us a clue.*

"Oh, yeah," Casey wiped his hands on the front of his T-shirt. "You look nice."

"Nice?" Mom made a face. "That's what someone says to you when you don't."

Dylan flicked his ears. *Why is all your hair on top of your head?*

Casey scrambled for something else to say, "You look *really* nice. Right, Little Buddy?" He shifted Dylan on the couch, so they could get a better look at the TV.

Dylan watched Doc Brown, a crazy old guy with frizzy white hair, trying to hook something like a thick rope up to a clock tower in a storm. Behind him lightning cracked and broke through the night sky. *You'd better hurry up, Doc.*

"Yeah, Ms. D. Really nice." Sumo took another slice of pizza from the box on the coffee table. It almost made it to his mouth before a glop of marinara sauce landed on his shirt.

Dylan looked Mom up and down. *You're wearing a nightgown.*

Sumo swiped at the sauce with his finger and licked it clean. "Why are you wearing a white dress to a barbecue?"

Her shoulders slumped. She looked to the ceiling before giving them a patient smile. "*Hieronymus the Hamster Goes to Nasa's* book launch party is tonight."

"Yeah," Casey and Sumo said.

Even I know that.

"Oddly enough, Nasa is the theme for the party. All guests are to wear white. You know, like the white space suit Hieronymus painted in his book."

Dylan stretched out his paws and looked himself over. *Casey says I'm blond. That's almost white.*

"I managed to borrow exhibits from the 50th anniversary of Apollo 11's moon landing. The space suits worn by astronauts Buzz Aldrin and Neil Armstrong will be on display."

"Oh, man." Sumo shoved the pizza into his mouth and mumbled, "I gotta see the space suits. I wish we could try them on."

That dumb hamster Hieronymus painted a bunch of pictures of a man in a puffy suit with a big bubble on his head. Dylan looked at Mom's sleeveless long white dress. *You don't look like an astronaut.*

"Do we get food at this thing?" Casey gave Dylan a little bit of crust with cheese.

Don't be stingy. Dylan put his muzzle Casey's thigh and slid his tongue sideways onto his plate, sliding past the bell peppers and icky things Casey called bean sprouts. He snagged a mushroom. *Not bad.*

"Yes. The barbecue starts at seven o'clock, but servers will be greeting guests with appetizers before that."

Casey and Sumo did a high-five. Casey and Dylan did a down low.

Mom stayed in front of the TV screen. "I'm going to meet Jonah and Anna at the Brea Country Club now. What will you be doing?"

Casey moved to his left and gestured to the big screen with his pizza. "We're watching a *Back to the Future* movie marathon."

"Doc Brown built a time machine out of a cool car called a DeLorean." Sumo raised his cell phone. "I googled DeLorean. The cars were only made from 1981 to 1983. The doors went up and down. Have you seen the movies?"

Doc Brown has a big, furry dog named Einstein. Maybe I could be in a movie.

She turned to look at the screen and laughed. "Only about ten times. Remember to be at Brea Country Club by three o'clock. You'll need time to change into your uniforms."

"Aw, Mom. Why do we have to wear stupid uniforms?"

"That's how the guests will know you're working for Brea's Ice Cream."

Dylan wiggled forward and hooked his paws over the edge of the couch. *What about me?*

"Dylan will wear his Dream Big bandana." She thought for a moment. "Hmm. Dream Big. I'm getting an excellent marketing idea."

Sumo held up his cell phone, showing the time. "It's getting late, Ms. D."

"One more thing, boys." She handed Casey a typed, single-spaced, one-page paper. "This is today's agenda."

Sumo leaned over Dylan and looked at it. "Is it alphabetized?"

Casey skimmed over it. "Nah. It's by time, starting a three o'clock." He waved it in the air. "This is a lot of stuff. Which part is ours?"

She took the paper back and held it up. "I've highlighted your part in yellow." She pointed to the fourth line. "Leave house by two-thirty." Her finger went to the fifth line. "Arrive at Brea Country Club by two-fifty."

Casey snatched the paper back and counted. "There's thirty-seven things highlighted here. Where's the part where we get to go home?"

"Dylan is finished at seven o'clock. Start cleaning up by six forty-five, so you can get him and be home before it gets dark."

"Okay." Casey tossed the paper onto the couch, where it slid off and onto the floor. "No problem."

"I'll come by and see you throughout the event. If you have any questions, just text me. At six o'clock, I'll be at the book signing table with Gina, Priscilla, and Teri. Be sure you say goodbye before you go home."

"Okay."

"Okay." Mom took a deep breath, crossed her second

and third fingers on both hands and held them up. "Wish me luck."

"Good luck, Mom."

Arf!

"Thanks." Mom gave a little wave. "Oh, and take your feet off the coffee table," she called back over her shoulder.

Dylan kicked out his paws. *My feet don't reach the coffee table.*

Dylan went back to the movie. Marty, the kid in the movie was sleeping in bed and drooling on his pillow. When Marty woke up and went outside, Doc Brown was waiting. They hopped into the DeLorean and zoomed off to the future.

What about Einstein?

"Oh, man," Sumo rubbed his stomach. "I don't feel so good."

"Serves you right," Casey tossed his empty plate into the pizza box, "for pigging out."

"You're jealous because my pizza was better."

"Am not."

Dylan licked Sumo's plate. *Was, too.*

Sumo checked his cell phone. "What time did your mom say we had to be there?"

"Four o'clock."

"Are you sure it's not three o'clock? Maybe you should check the paper."

"Nah. She always gets all nervous about this book stuff and it always works out. I've been to a ton of these." Casey picked up the remote. "We've got plenty of time for the next movie."

"Yeah?"

"Yeah."

I don't think so.

FOURTEEN

"Peddle faster!"

"I am!" Sumo leaned forward on his bike. "I can't believe we're late."

I can. Dylan looked out the side screens of his bike trailer and watched lawn and trees whiz by. Casey made a sharp turn. The bike and its trailer teetered and then struggled down a gravel driveway. Dylan's head bumped, bumped, bumped against the fabric ceiling of the trailer. *Ow.*

When Casey skidded the bike to a stop next to a guard shack, Dylan flew forward and his ears flopped over his face. *Hey!*

A woman with a granite face stepped out of the guard shack, held up an iPad and growled, "Let's see some identification." Her name tag read Brunhilda.

Casey hooked a thumb over his shoulder at Sumo. "We're twelve. We don't have any identification."

Brunhilda frowned. "Who are you?"

"Casey Donovan and Sumo Modragon. My mom is Colleen Donovan and she's in charge of this book launch."

Sumo brought his bike next to Casey's. "Hi."

Brunhilda checked the guest list on her iPad. "I've worked here twenty-five years and I've seen it all." She gnashed her teeth. "But tonight, takes the cake. A book launch for a hamster."

I know. Really.

She walked around their bikes and stopped at Casey's bike trailer. "What's in this?"

Whine. Dylan pawed the screen.

"My dog." Casey grinned. "His collar has an ID tag. That should make you happy."

It didn't. "Dogs aren't allowed at the Brea Country Club. Uh-uh." She shook her head left and right like a metronome. "No way he's coming in here."

"Yeah, he is." Casey got off his bike and unzipped the front screen on the trailer. "He's doing photo ops tonight."

"He's famous," Sumo said.

"A dog is doing photo ops. That's a good one." She rolled her eyes. "That's right up there with having a book launch for a hamster." Brunhilda bent down and looked inside. "Dylan!" She put her iPad on the ground. "I know you. You're Dylan! I'm a member of Dylan's Dog Squad. I follow you on social media." She reached inside and petted his ears. "You found the little boy at the mall."

Dylan licked her hand. *It was nothing.*

She turned his bandana around. "Dream Big. That says it all. You're a hero."

"Dylan's doing photo ops," Casey said again. "Maybe you can come by later."

Brunhilda beamed. "I'll be there."

Casey looked around. "Can you tell me where we're supposed to go?"

"Of course. Happy to help." She stood up, studied her

iPad, and showed Casey the map. "Brea's Ice Cream is here. Dominick and Crystal are setting up." She rotated her iPad. "Anna the photographer is set up by the Milky Way display. That's here." Brunhilda arched her eyebrows and leaned in, suddenly his best friend. "You're late. Ms. Donovan has been calling every fifteen minutes. Want me to tell her you're here?"

"That's okay. Where is she?"

Brunhilda swiped at the screen. "She and the writer and illustrators are already set up on the north side of the lawn. Book signing is at six o'clock." She checked another screen. "Your mother and Jonah, that handsome newspaper man," she patted her steel grey curls, "are mingling with the crowd." She tried a smile and a gold-capped tooth winked. "Do you think you can get Jonah to put my name in his newspaper story?"

"Sure thing. You're a friend of Dylan's."

A flash of pink washed over her face, and she sent them through the gate with a little finger wave.

"Next," she barked to the car behind them. "Let's see some identification."

Casey and Sumo parked their bikes in the guest parking lot next to a small, paneled truck with a Mike's Party Company logo on its side. The back doors were open, and a guy was struggling to get a table out.

Casey called, "Want some help?"

"I've got it." He pushed his baseball cap up and wiped his forehead with the back of his hand. "Thanks anyway."

Sumo got off his bike and looked around. "There's already a ton of people here. You could tell your mom we got here a long time ago."

Are you kidding? Mom knows everything.

"You heard Brunhilda. She's been calling every fifteen

minutes." Casey texted her. "That should do it." Casey got
Dylan out of the bike trailer and smoothed his topknot away
from his eyes. "C'mon, Little Buddy, let's go see Anna. Can
you find Dominick and Crystal and tell them I'll be over
soon?"

"Okay."

Casey and Dylan dodged servers carrying platters of
food. They detoured across the lawn roped off for the
barbecue and passed a gigantic white canopy tent. Two
bartenders were inside, stocking the bar and arranging
champagne glasses. Outside four chefs worked over large
grills fueled by hot coals, poking at beef with tongs, too busy
to pay attention to a boy and a dog. Casey sniffed. "The
guests are getting tri-tip tonight."

Dylan inhaled. *I hope I'm getting tri-tip.* He cocked his
head and looked up at Casey. *Is tri-tip steak?*

They hustled past rows of tables draped in midnight
blue tablecloths and scattered with crystal pieces. "Mom
did a good job with the tables." Casey stopped and lifted
Dylan up. "The crystals make them look like the Milky
Way."

Pretty. What's the Milky Way?

"Over here, Casey and Dylan." Anna was fussing with a
backdrop of midnight blue splashed with sparkly stars. In
front of the backdrop stood a midnight blue pedestal
holding a massive, revolving ice sculpture. Inside the sculpture was a globe of the earth. Its continents and oceans in
brilliant colors shone through the ice. Behind a velvet rope,
men and women wearing white were lined up, waiting to
have their picture taken.

"Mom really outdid herself with the ice sculpture,"
Casey said to Anna, "but isn't she afraid the thing will
melt?"

Anna laughed. "Colleen says the ice sculpture is *guaranteed* by Ice Magic. If it lasts until six forty-five, we're fine. That's when the faery lights are scheduled to come on." She pointed to the thousands of lights strung above their heads and around the grounds. "When the lights come on, that's the signal for the band to play Fly Me to the Moon. The guests will be escorted to the barbecue area by volunteers dressed in white space suits."

"Nice."

"Your mom comes up with the best ideas. She told me to drape this padded platform with more of the midnight blue and sparkly stars material and put Dylan on it. When I take the picture of him with the guests, he'll look like he's floating in the Milky Way." She raised her Sony up. "I'll start taking pictures in a few minutes."

"Okay, Little Buddy." Casey settled him on the platform and rubbed under his muzzle. "Have a good time. I'll be back for you at seven o'clock." Casey raised his right hand, showing Dylan his little finger, index finger and thumb.

Arf! Arf!

"I heard you and Dylan have been learning sign language. What was that?"

Casey raised his hand and gave the sign again. "I love you."

"Always good to know."

"We've been working on directions." Casey raised his left hand and showed Dylan his left thumb and index finger and moved it left. "That means left." Casey raised his right hand, crossed his index and third finger, and waved it right. "That means right."

Arf! Arf! Arf!

"Okay, Little Buddy." Casey laughed and reached into

his pocket for the treat bag. "That means Dylan gets three treats."

Dylan licked Casey's hand and stretched out. *Save me some ice cream.*

Casey trotted across the lawn to Brea's Ice Cream station. Sumo was already behind the counter, and he gave Casey the hurry up sign. When Casey passed the long display case, he felt a wave of cold air coming from it. He stopped, shook his sticky shirt away from his skin and closed his eyes. "Feels good."

"Hi." A college-looking guy took off his wire-rimmed glasses, wiped them on the edge of his plaid vest and then put them back on. "I'm Dominick."

"Hi, I'm Crystal." A short girl with short, spiky red hair disappeared behind the display case, came up with a plaid vest, and handed it to him. "Here."

Sumo was already wearing his. He pulled at the baggy vest. "These look dumb."

"Real dumb." Casey tried handing it back.

"Uh-uh," Dominick said. "If we have to wear them, so do you."

"Okay, fine." Casey put it on. "What do you want us to do?"

Crystal gave them two pairs of gloves. "Wash your hands and put these on."

They did.

"We have twelve flavors tonight," Dominick began, starting at one end of the display case. "All the fixings are on the long table over there along with napkins and spoons."

Crystal tied an apron around her waist. "The good news is you can eat as much ice cream as you want."

"Really?" Sumo got happy. "I'm starving."

"The featured ice creams," Dominick tapped a sign on

top of the ice cream display case, "are listed here. We've got Moon Rocks."

"What's that?" Casey peered into the display case.

"It's really Rocky Road. This one is Sunbeam." He motioned in the direction of a pale orange tub. "It's really mango sherbet."

"Then there's Moonlight." Crystal put on a pair of gloves and reached for an ice cream scoop.

Sumo pointed. "Why does it have white sticks in it?"

"That's coconut." Crystal waved her scoop at a tub filled with blah beige ice cream, black nuggets, and chunks of something shriveled up and dark brown, "This is Hamster Trail Mix. My favorite."

"What's that?" Casey's upper lip curled.

Dominick shook his head. "You don't want to know."

"Okay," Sumo and Casey raised their hands and backed up.

Two ladies with kids drifted their way. Crystal waved them over. "We're open, folks. What will it be?"

After that the crowd was nonstop. An hour later, Sumo griped, "We're so busy I can hardly eat any ice cream."

"Feels like we've been doing this all day." Casey filled a dish with three scoops of something purple and handed it to a little girl. When Mom and Jonah showed up, Casey almost leaped over the counter to say hello.

"We just saw Dylan." Mom sighed happily. "He is stealing the show. I had no idea how many people followed him on social media."

Sumo checked his cell phone and tapped something. "His public is interested. He gets hundreds of hits a day. People asking questions. People posting Dylan sightings."

Casey laughed. "You'll have him running for President soon."

Sumo's head jerked up. "What about school elections? I could start the campaign now."

Mom gave the time out signal. "I really came by to ask how it's going." She quickly counted the people standing in line behind her. "Looks like the ice cream is a hit."

"You'd think they never had ice cream before," Casey grumbled, rubbing his sore shoulder.

Jonah walked up and down the display case. "Which one do you recommend?"

"Not the Hamster Trail Mix," Casey and Sumo said together.

Mom studied the tub of ice cream. "What are those shriveled up brown things?"

"You don't want to know," Dominick whispered.

Five people ordered cups of the Hamster Trail Mix.

Crystal scooped up the ice cream and handed the cups to the guests. "It's been the most popular." She tapped the scoop against the rim of the ice cream bin. "We're almost out."

Mom held up her cell phone. "Smile, Sumo."

"Why?"

"I love the plaid vest." She checked the picture on her phone. "This is how I imagine Cranston looked like as a boy. I'm sending this picture to the illustrators to give them some ideas for his book."

"Aw, Ms. D."

Casey laughed and held up his cell phone. "We should hear from Dylan's Dog Squad."

"Gimme that!"

Casey danced back. "Hey, you're always posting pictures of me and Dylan on social media."

Sumo yanked at his vest. "But you weren't wearing this stupid thing in those pictures."

"No, but you are in this one." Casey grinned, waving his cell phone.

"Enough," Mom jumped in, but she was laughing. "Jonah and I need to check on the band. Be sure to stop by the book signing table before you go home."

Sumo waited for her to leave before punching Casey in the arm.

"Ow." Casey rubbed his arm. "You'll have to scoop my ice cream for me."

"Shut up."

At six forty-five, the faery lights began to twinkle in the dusky night and the band launched into Fly Me to the Moon.

"That's our cue." Dominick put up the Closed sign on top of the ice cream display case.

"Aw." "C'mon." "We want ice cream."

"Sorry. That's it, folks."

Volunteers in white space suits appeared and began herding guests away from the ice cream station. "Please come with us to the white canopy tent where champagne is being served." They pointed to the far lawn where chefs were working the grills. "The barbecue will be ready soon."

Casey stretched his back out and rolled his shoulders. "I'm never scooping ice cream again."

"I'm never eating ice cream again." Sumo rubbed his stomach. "Not today anyway."

Casey pulled out his cell phone and checked it. "I can't believe Mom only texted four times. She must be doing okay."

Sumo took off his vest and threw it on the counter behind him. "Remember to tell her when we leave."

"Yeah." Casey took off his vest and tossed it on top of

Sumo's. "The book signing started about forty-five minutes ago."

"Did you save Dylan some ice cream?"

Casey showed him a tiny bit of vanilla ice cream in a junior cup. "Absolutely."

"Thanks for all your help, guys," Crystal said. "I'm glad to go home. My feet hurt."

"Yeah." Dominick raked his hands over his eyes. "I'm going to have nightmares about ice cream for a week."

Casey pointed to the little round tables in front of the ice cream display. "Do we need to break down the tables or do anything with the tablecloths?"

Crystal got her car keys out of her purse. "Your mom hired Mike's Party Company." She jutted her chin toward his truck in the guest parking lot. "They'll take care of it."

"I have to go," Sumo said. "My mom is driving to Paso Robles tonight, and I promised to be home before she leaves."

"Okay." Casey waved goodbye and walked over to Anna and Dylan.

"How's my Little Buddy?" Casey ruffled Dylan's ears. "Look what I brought you."

Ice cream! Dylan stretched up into a sitting position and stuck his muzzle into the cup. He licked the ice cream so hard Casey nearly dropped it.

"Hey, you got some on your nose."

Dylan shot his long pink tongue out and up. *All gone.*

"Everybody loved Dylan," Anna said, stroking his back. "I had a hard time getting them to leave after I took their picture."

"Have you seen my mom?"

"She came by twice. Once with Jonah and once with

Mayor Matias. She's doing the book signing with Teri, Priscilla and Gina now."

"I forgot! I'm supposed to tell her when I leave." Casey scanned the crowd. "There's got to be five hundred people here. Dylan, stay with Anna and I'll be right back, okay?"

"Sure. He's fine."

Casey lifted Dylan off the padded platform and put him on the ground. "You can stretch your legs while Anna packs up. I'll be back in a minute."

Dylan began circling the backdrop, sniffing for crumbs. *There must be something.*

Anna got her backpack out and started dismantling her camera table.

"Hey, Anna."

She looked up. "Hi, Mike. This was quite the night."

His arms were loaded with tablecloths. "Now it's time to get this side of it cleaned up." He turned to the white canopy tent where guests were sipping champagne. "The barbecue is about to start. Do you mind if I drop these here? I want to get my truck closer. It'll make loading up easier."

"No problem."

Mike dropped the tablecloths on the ground and took off across the lawn.

All night Dylan had seen people walking around eating food way too big for the little napkins they used to carry it. He scouted around in the grass and found some cheese and crackers. *It's a start.* Someone had dropped a teeny, tiny turkey sandwich. *One measly bite.* Dylan sniffed behind the velvet rope where people had stood in line waiting to have their picture taken. Something was in the grass, and he pawed at it. A row of olives and tomatoes on a toothpick popped up. He dropped to his stomach and held it between his paws. The olives and tomatoes were too hard to get off the toothpick, so he munched the whole thing.

Dylan circled around the Milky Way display, but he hadn't missed anything. *People shouldn't use napkins when they eat.* A cool wind blew, and he lifted his muzzle, feeling his ears blow away from his face. A big yawn came out of nowhere. *I'm ready for a nap. Where is Casey? All I see are legs, legs, and more legs hurrying to get to the barbecue.*

"Excuse us." A man and woman came up to Anna.

"We're sorry to bother you," the man said.

"No problem." Anna put her camera on the table. "What can I do for you?"

The woman fluttered her hands in the air. "You took our picture earlier. It was perfect, so we wanted to show it to our friends. Somehow," the hands were back in the air, "I managed to delete the digital copy you sent to us."

The man put his arm around her shoulders. "Is it possible to get another copy?"

"Of course." Anna picked up her camera and started searching. "This won't take long."

Dylan padded over to the tablecloths on the lawn. He sniffed at them. *No food. Sad.* He worked the tablecloths with his paws until they were comfy, and he plopped down. *This feels soft like the cushion in my bike trailer.* Dylan put his muzzle on his front paws and closed his eyes. *Maybe a little snooze until Casey comes.*

Mike came over with another load of tablecloths and dropped them on top of the tablecloths on the ground. "I'm all set. Thanks, Anna."

Anna nodded and waved, still talking to the couple.

Mike bent down and picked up all the tablecloths—and Dylan.

FIFTEEN

Dylan opened his eyes and blinked. *It's dark.* Scooting his buns underneath him, he spread his paws out in front and gripped the soft cloth. *I'm moving but I'm not in my bike trailer.* Panic squeezed Dylan's heart. *Where's Casey? I'm scared.*

Dylan raised his snout and sniffed. *Nothing.* He sank his nose into the cloth and inhaled. *Smells like grass. Oh-oh. These must be the tablecloths the man put on the ground next to Anna. The ones I took a nap on.*

He tried using his paws to push into a sitting position, but his chain collar caught on the soft tablecloth. Throwing back his head, he wiggled in reverse taking the tablecloth with him. He put his head down again, dug in with his back paws, and gave it all he had. His chain collar and bandana slipped over his ears, sending Dylan flying back on his rump.

Dylan rubbed his ear with his back paw and got to his feet. He was getting used to the darkness but not his fear. He looked around. *I'm in a truck. It's crowded with tables, folding chairs, and boxes. Where am I going? Can Casey find me?*

The truck eased to a stop and Dylan's ears pricked. He heard a door slam and then footsteps. *Oh no.* He looked around. *Nowhere to hide.*

The rollup door groaned open.

Dylan saw a man standing in the shadows. *Will you hurt me?*

The man reached for the tablecloths and then hesitated.

No! My collar and bandana are in there.

The man whispered to himself. "It's late. They can wait until tomorrow." He started to roll the door down but stopped. "Who's there?"

Dylan backed up as far as he could, his buns pushed against a box, and he shut his eyes. *You can't see me if my eyes are closed.*

The man climbed into the truck and crouched down in front of Dylan. "What are you doing here?"

I'm lost.

The man reached out and petted Dylan's head. "It's okay. You're safe."

Dylan didn't budge.

"I'm not going to hurt you."

The man's hands were rough, but his voice was soft.

Luca got lost. I found him. Who will find me?

"Let's go inside. It's been a long day." The man waited. He put his hands under Dylan's stomach and lifted him up, bringing him close to his chest. "That's not so bad, is it?"

I don't know.

The man hopped down, out of the truck. "Are you hungry? I am." He turned around and tugged on the truck's pull-down door handle.

No! Dylan hooked his front paws over the man's shoulders and kicked out with his back paws. *I need my collar and bandana!*

"It's okay." The man walked toward a little house with the front porch light on.

"Hello, Mike."

"Hi, Mrs. Porter." The man pushed past the older woman and stood in the foyer. "We have a guest for dinner."

"I see." The woman's face, as round and as soft as a biscuit, leaned closer. "Where did he come from?"

"I found him in the truck. He must be lost. He doesn't have a collar."

Yes, I do!

"Poor thing." She ran her hands down Dylan's ears and along his back. "He doesn't look like a stray. He must belong to someone."

I belong to Casey.

"It's late. I'll make some calls tomorrow."

Call Casey!

Mrs. Porter gave Dylan's shoulders a small pat. "You'll be all right." She untied her apron and folded it over her arm. "I've left your dinner in the oven. It's warm."

"Thanks. Is Amy asleep?"

"Yes."

Mike shifted Dylan in his arms. "How many stories did you have to read?"

"Only three." Mrs. Porter smiled. "She's always a good girl."

"Thanks again, Mrs. Porter." Mike opened the door and followed her onto the porch. "We'll wait here and watch you go inside your house."

Mrs. Porter nodded and took off down the walk, crossing the street. When she reached the front door of her house, she turned and waved.

"I know you must be as hungry as I am," Mike said, stepping inside the house, "but I need to look in on Amy first."

Dylan rested his head on the man's shoulder. *I'm scared. I'm tired. And I'm lost. What's an Amy?*

At the end of the hall a door stood slightly ajar. Mike pushed gently against the door with his index finger, and they stepped inside. In the shadows of a Cinderella bed lamp on low, a little girl was sleeping. She clutched a doll to her chest. Mike smiled at Dylan. He stepped back into the hall, almost closing the door, and whispered, "She'll be five tomorrow."

When they got to the kitchen, Mike put Dylan on the rug in front of the sink. He reached into a cupboard, found a bowl, and filled it with water. "Thirsty?"

Dylan put his muzzle in the bowl and drank it all. When he finished, he licked the bowl and looked up at Mike.

Mike scratched Dylan on his head. "Let's wait a bit and then I'll give you some more. I don't want you to get sick." He opened a drawer, took out two oven mitts and put them on.

Mom has oven mitts. Dylan's heart hurt to beat. *Will I ever see Mom and Casey again?*

Dylan followed Mike over to the oven and watched while he pulled a big pan out. Good smells filled the kitchen and his stomach growled. Steam from the open oven fogged up the kitchen windows.

Mike hip bumped the oven door shut and he put the pan on top of the stove. He leaned closer and sniffed. "I have no idea what this is. Mrs. Porter never makes the same thing twice." He got a big spoon out of the drawer and moved things around. "Looks like beef, veggies and brown gravy. Want to try it?"

Whine.

He got two bowls out of the cupboard and filled one. "This is really hot. Hold on." He put the bowl in the fridge. "Only for a minute. I don't want you to burn your tongue." Mike fixed himself a bowl, found some bread in a plastic bag on the counter, and motioned for Dylan to follow him to the table.

Dylan raced ahead. *I'm hungry.*

When Mike went back to the kitchen, Dylan trotted along beside him. Dylan watched him take the bowl out of the fridge and stick his finger in the middle.

"Perfect. Not too hot. C'mon." Mike took the bowl to the dining room and set it down in front of Dylan. "Try it."

Dylan sniffed, licked, and then woofed it down. *Not Mom's but not bad.*

Mike dug in. "I'm glad you liked it." He picked up the bread and broke off a piece for Dylan. "Mrs. Porter takes care of Amy when I'm working."

Dylan stopped chewing. *You sound sad.*

He wiped his mouth with a paper napkin. "My wife got sick. It's just the two of us now." He took a bite of the bread and gave Dylan another nibble. "Amy is going to be so excited to see you tomorrow. She really wants a dog."

Dylan's internal elevator dropped a few floors. *I really want Casey.*

Mike gave him the rest of the bread. He got up and came back with another bowl of water. "Finish this up. It's time to get some sleep."

SIXTEEN

"Hi," Carl called. He and Dempsey hurried across the lawn to join Casey, Mom, Rory, and Anna. "We came as soon as we heard."

"Thanks." Rory rubbed his forehead. "We've done all we can."

"What can we do to help?"

"This is all my fault," Anna sobbed and knuckled her eyes. "I was supposed to watch Dylan, but I got distracted. A couple lost their picture and needed a replacement. When I finished with them, Dylan was gone. I'm sorry, Casey."

"Things happen." Rory put a hand on her shoulder. "It was dark. Dylan probably wandered off and got turned around."

"No way," Casey interrupted. "Dylan's smart and he's a Velcro dog. I tell him to stay, and he stays."

"Casey's right," Mom agreed. "Dylan would never leave on his own."

Carl nodded to Mom. "What have you done so far?"

"We've made announcements and cadets are searching the grounds." She sighed. "No one has seen him."

"Dempsey, ready to go to work?" Carl held out both hands, closed them into fists and then tapped his right hand on top of his left wrist two times. "Dempsey, work."

Arf! Dempsey leaned against Carl and rubbed his head against his thigh.

"Casey, do you have something of Dylan's?"

"This is his blanket from the bike trailer." Casey handed it over.

Mom bit her lip. "Can Dempsey find Dylan in the dark?"

"Sis," Rory said, "if Dylan left a trail, Dempsey can track him."

Carl brought Dylan's blanket close to Dempsey's nose. "This is Dylan. Find Dylan."

Arf! Dempsey raised his big head and scented the air. He dropped his nose to the ground and started walking toward the table Anna had used for her camera equipment. Carl followed closely behind him. Dempsey stopped and alerted. *Arf!*

"Good boy," Carl said. "He's got the scent." He gave Dylan's blanket to him again. "This is Dylan. Find Dylan."

Carl and Dempsey veered off to the backdrop and then over to the velvet ropes. Again, Dempsey alerted.

Dempsey went up and down the velvet ropes before retracing his steps and going back to Anna's table. He plopped his big buns on the ground and focused on Carl. *Arf!*

"What does Dempsey mean," asked Anna.

Carl extended both arms up with his index fingers pointed toward Dempsey. He bent his arms at the elbows, pulling his fingers toward his body. "Come." Dempsey ambled over to Carl. Carl patted his head and gave him a treat. "I'm sorry, folks. That's the end of the trail. Dempsey hasn't lost the scent. He's saying there isn't any more scent."

"Dylan's vanished?" Mom put her hand to her mouth. "From that spot? That's impossible."

"Uncle Rory, we've got to keep looking." Casey's voice hitched, "Dylan's lost."

"It's too dark." Rory turned away and spoke into his radio. After a minute he clicked off and faced his sister. "Colleen, I told everyone to call it a night. I'm sorry." He turned to Anna. "You should go home, too."

"Okay," she sniffed. "I'm so sorry. Bye."

Mom's cell phone vibrated. She read it and then showed it to Rory. "Sumo says he's got Dylan's Dog Squad on this. They're canvassing the surrounding neighborhood with flashlights. Someone named Brunhilda is in charge." She started to send a reply but stopped and looked up. "Is there really someone named Brunhilda?"

"Oh, yeah." Rory nodded fast. "Brunhilda's scary but she's good. She's been running the guard shack at the Brea Country Club for as long as I can remember. No one gets past her that shouldn't. She's already checked the outgoing logs for us and sent over the footage from the cameras. So far, everyone and everything matches."

"I don't get it, Uncle Rory." Casey held his hands out to his sides and did a one-eighty turn. "It was like a small city here tonight. Dylan is famous. Wouldn't someone wonder why he was by himself?"

"People were having a good time. Face it," Rory took a step back from his sister, "Dylan's short. Most people don't look down."

Casey fisted his hands. "We can't stand around doing nothing. Dylan's got to be so scared."

"Why give up now?" Carl jiggled Dempsey's leash. "We've got all night. Right, Dempsey?"

Arf!

"All right." Rory huffed out a breath and checked his watch. "I'm off duty. Let's go look for Dylan."

SEVENTEEN

Dylan heard Amy before he saw her coming.

"Daddy!" She bounced into the kitchen. "Sophie says she's not coming to my birthday party because I wore a pink shirt at the playground yesterday and Ella has one just like it and it hurt Ella's feelings and," Amy skidded to a stop. "Oh!"

Dylan flicked his ears. *I don't know what you said but I know I liked you better asleep.*

"Daddy!" She was on Dylan in a flash and had him in a chokehold. "You got me a puppy for my birthday."

Arrghf! Dylan tried wiggling in reverse, but no luck. *Help! The kid has a death grip on me.*

Mike reached down and pried Amy's arms away from around Dylan's neck. "You have to be gentle with him. He's a puppy."

She lunged for Dylan again, grabbed his muzzle with both hands and gave him smoochy, lip-smacking kisses. "I love him. Mine, mine, mine."

Yuck! Dylan scooted away. He tried opening and shutting his mouth a few times. *Still works.*

"Amy," Mike came down to her size. "I know you want a puppy, but this puppy belongs to someone else."

Tears filled her eyes and pink lips blubbered. "Why?"

"I found him in my truck last night." Mike dragged Dylan over. "Look at his nice fur. Someone took good care of him. I bet that someone is looking for him right now."

You tell her, Mike.

Tears turned to tyranny. "They lost him. Finders keepers, losers weepers."

Huh?

Mike smiled. "How would you feel if you lost your Ariel doll, and someone found it? Wouldn't you want that person to give her back to you?"

Listen to your dad, kid.

Amy crossed her arms and tapped her small foot. "I wouldn't lose her in the first place."

You're losing the fight here, Mike.

"The right thing to do," Mike continued, "is to try to find his owner. I have work to do this morning, but I'll make some calls later. I'm thinking he belongs to someone from the book launch last night."

Keep thinking, Mike.

Mike stood up. "Right now, it's breakfast time."

About time. Dylan's stomach growled. Mom's Breakfast of Champions were the best. They were always something fluffy, like fluffy eggs or fluffy pancakes or fluffy muffins. *I like them all.*

Mike reached behind him for two boxes on the counter and held them up. "Pink or blue?"

Amy clapped her tiny hands. "Pink! Pink!"

What's with all the pink?

Dylan padded into the dining room and sat by Mike's chair. *Ready.*

Amy climbed onto the chair next to him. The dining room table came up to her chin.

A few minutes later Mike brought in two glasses of orange juice. "Be back."

On his next trip, he added two glasses of chocolate milk. "Almost ready."

Dylan danced in place. *Breakfast must be really yummy if it's taking this long.*

This time Mike carried in a large plate and put it in the center of the table. He grabbed a rectangle thing off the top, showed it to Dylan, and winked. "Look what I have for you."

Looks like cardboard with something smeared on top. Pink?

Mike held it out for Dylan. "Strawberry Pop-Tart."

Dylan studied it. He sniffed it. He looked at Mike. *Do you know how much sugar is in that?*

"Go ahead."

Dylan leaned forward to take the Pop-Tart in one bite and all forty-two teeth sank in. *Agh!* He tried throwing his head back and giving it a few quick chomps. The thing stuck out on either side of his muzzle.

He dropped to his stomach, drooling. Rolling side-to-side, the Pop-Tart broke and fell out. Dylan pawed at the pieces. *It's like bits of wood.*

Dylan looked at Amy. She was holding one with both hands and nibbling around the edges.

"How do you like it," Mike asked.

Dylan's stomach growled again. *I hate it.* He licked at a piece. It softened and stuck to his tongue. *Can you ask Mrs. Porter to fix breakfast?*

During breakfast Mike didn't talk much, and Amy talked nonstop.

I'm tired of listening. Dylan curled up and thought of Casey and Mom. *I need to get home, but where's home?* Dylan thought some more. *Mike knows about the book launch, so he must have been at the Brea Country Club last night. I don't think I was in his truck for very long, so Mike must live close to the Brea Country Club.* Hope rose in his heart like a big red balloon. *If I could get to the Brea Country Club, maybe I could get home.*

Dylan's plan began to take shape. *Brunhilda works at the Brea Country Club. She knows me. She could help me.* Dylan looked around the house. *No open doors. No open windows. There must be a way out of here.*

"I'm sorry, Amy," Mike was saying, "I have to work this morning."

"No." Amy kicked her short legs under the table and the waterworks began. "Stay home."

Dylan blinked. *What did I miss?*

"I promise I'll be back in time for your birthday party." The doorbell rang, and Mike scooted his chair back. "That's Mrs. Porter. She'll stay with you until I get home. She's going to help you put on your princess dress." Mike stood and tugged on Amy's curls. "You'll be the prettiest princess at the party."

Mike went to answer the door and Dylan raced after him. When Mike opened the door, Dylan muscled between his legs and stuck his snout out. "Not so fast." Mike blocked Dylan's exit with his leg. "You'll get lost."

I'm already lost.

"Hi, Mike." Mrs. Porter came in, carrying a box. They followed her into the dining room.

"Happy birthday, Amy." She lowered the box for Amy to see. "Look, I have the tiaras for your birthday party."

Dylan stretched up on his hind legs for a look inside. *Sparkly. Nice.*

"Yay! Which one is mine?"

Mrs. Porter smiled. "The pink one, of course."

Dylan dropped down to the ground. *They all look the same.*

"You are so cute." Mrs. Porter gave Dylan a friendly pat and turned to Mike. "I see you still have the dog."

"My dog," Amy insisted. "His name is Prince because I'm Princess Amy, and today is my birthday."

Mike heaved a sigh. "I've tried telling Amy that Prince must belong to someone." He kissed the top of Amy's head. "I'll be back soon. Sara and Duncan will be here in a few minutes to set up the backyard for the party. They're also bringing the cake and the food. Thanks, Mrs. Porter."

"Of course."

Dylan followed Mike to the front door. *Take me with you.*

"This should be quite the day." Mike ran a hand through his hair. "Thank goodness for Mrs. Porter. I'm not sure if I could handle four little girls hyped up on sugar and dressed like princesses." He smiled. "Amy is so excited."

I'm not.

"Stay here," Mike said. "I'll be back after I empty the truck and take the tablecloths to the dry cleaners."

No! Dylan scratched at Mike's leg. *My collar and bandana are with the tablecloths.*

"Don't worry. I promise to be back in time to save you." Mike opened the door a crack and slipped out.

Dylan got to his hind feet and pawed the doorknob. *It's round and too slippery for me to open.* He sank down to all fours and scratched one ear with his back paw. *There must be a way.*

Dylan padded back to the kitchen and found Mrs. Porter and Amy making lemonade.

"Put in lots and lots of strawberries," Amy directed, pointing to a clear bowl. "I want really, really pink lemonade."

Mrs. Porter cut the last strawberry and tipped a cutting board loaded with them into the bowl. She laughed. "It's pink."

I really must find out what pink is.

Amy's forehead wrinkled. "Will my birthday cake be pink?"

Ask me! Dylan raised one paw. *I know! I know!*

"Yes, Princess Amy." Mrs. Porter wiped her hands on a kitchen towel and pulled her into a hug. "The cake is pink. The frosting is pink, and it's trimmed with oodles of strawberries."

"Okay." Happiness reigned briefly. "What about pink ice cream?"

"Yes. Strawberry." Mrs. Porter rolled her eyes. "I took care of it myself."

"Okay."

The doorbell rang and Mrs. Porter checked the kitchen clock. "That must be Sara and Duncan."

Dylan darted past her and slid to a stop in front of the door. *Here's my chance.*

"Wait." Mrs. Porter's sturdy leg pinned Dylan to the side, but he wrapped his neck around the door and peeked out.

"Oh, how cute." Sara knelt and ran a hand over Dylan's ears.

"Mike found him last night. We have to be careful because he lost his collar."

Did not.

Sara waved a hand in the direction of the van. "I've got the cake and the food. I'll put them in the kitchen." She pointed to the side of the house. "Duncan is unloading the tables for the party. We'll go around back and set up. Mike gave us everything."

"Wonderful. Call if you need help."

Mrs. Porter closed the door on Dylan's escape. He trudged alongside her, his heart growing heavier with each step. *Mrs. Porter's old. It should've been easy to get out.*

"Princess Amy," Mrs. Porter called, "time to get you dressed."

Dylan saw a blur of girl and blonde curls shoot down the hallway. When they got to her bedroom, Amy was kicking off her shoes.

Mrs. Porter took a frilly dress off its hanger and smoothed out its long skirt. Amy tossed off her shirt and shorts and stood with her arms straight up in the air. After Mrs. Porter dropped the dress down over her head, Amy dashed over to the mirror. She used both hands to hold its skirt out and twirled.

"You look beautiful," Mrs. Porter's round face beamed.

Amy giggled.

"Mrs. Porter," a man's voice called from somewhere, "do you have a minute?"

"Coming, Duncan," she said. "Amy, you and Prince play. I'll be back."

Amy ran to her dresser and picked up her brush. "Bring back my tiara."

"I will."

Amy searched through a dresser drawer and took out a fistful of hair clips. "You're going to be beautiful, too."

She dropped the hair clips on the floor, pulled Dylan close and brushed his ears. "Your hair is curly like mine."

She chose a hair clip with flowers and ribbons. Grabbing the fur of one ear, she clipped it on. "There."

Ouch! Dylan shook his head until his teeth rattled, but the hair clip held on.

Amy hugged him and his eyes popped. "You really are a prince now."

I'm really running away.

EIGHTEEN

Mike rushed into the house and slammed the door. "Mrs. Porter! Amy! I'm late!"

No joke. Dylan charged into the foyer, did a bun burn on the tile floor, and skidded to a halt in front of Mike's feet. Dylan shook his head from side-to-side, but the dumb hair clip wouldn't fall out. *Notice anything?*

Mike patted Dylan on top of his head and walked around him.

Thanks a lot. Dylan followed him into the backyard anyway.

"Hi, Mike," Mrs. Porter called. "The girls are finishing lunch."

"Daddy!" Amy jumped up from the party table, ran across the lawn and hugged his legs. "Everybody came."

"Hello, princesses," Mike waved to the three little girls sitting at the table, eating sandwiches cut into triangles. Pink cream cheese and strawberry filling dripped out of the sandwiches and onto the pink plates. Glasses of pink lemonade were almost empty.

The princesses looked at him but kept eating. One

princess was wearing her tiara like a headband. Another had her tiara wrapped around her neck.

"Where were you? You promised you would be here." Princess Amy stamped a tiny foot in a sequined shoe.

Yeah, Mike. You promised.

"I know, Sweetheart. Are you mad at me?"

Amy's right shoe traced little circles on the grass. "Maybe."

"Too mad to see your surprise?"

Her mad was forgotten. "A surprise? Can I have it?"

The back gate opened, and Dylan took a step back. *Whoa! That is a very tall dog.*

"A horse!" "No, it's not." "It's a pony."

The man riding the dark brown horse brought him closer. "Happy birthday, Princess Amy."

For once, Amy's mouth didn't work.

"His name is Sir Galahad." Mike took her hand and showed her how to stroke the horse's flank. "Be gentle."

Three princesses jumped up from the table and ran over, squealing to be the first one to touch the horse. Sir Galahad whinnied and shifted in place.

"Can I ride him, Daddy?"

"Yes, you can ride him first. Then he will give the princesses a ride, too." Mike lifted her up and put her in front of the rider. "Jeremy will show you how to hold the reins."

Amy's small hands fumbled with the leather. "Like this?"

Mrs. Porter held up her cell phone. "Smile, Amy."

Mike held the horse's harness while Jeremey helped Amy with the reins.

The three little girls crowded in, all wanting a turn. "I'm next!" "Me!" "I saw him first."

Yip! Dylan stepped out of the way of six busy little feet. Dylan heard street sounds and when he turned, he saw the back gate was open.

His heart hitched. *Now's my chance.*

Dylan kept his eyes on Mike but slowly started backing up. *Don't look at me.*

"Princesses, picture time with Sir Galahad," Mrs. Porter insisted, motioning them in front of the horse. "Let's take a group picture."

Take lots of pictures. When Dylan reached the back gate, he bolted.

In the front yard, Dylan ran past the half-circle driveway and stopped on the sidewalk. The street was busy with cars. *Casey said never to cross the street, but how do I get home?* Dylan thought hard. Last night when Mike parked the truck in the driveway, the truck was facing the street. *Casey taught me that direction is right. We came from the other way. That's left.* Dylan turned left. *This is the way back to the Brea Country Club.*

I hope.

Dylan walked past houses and more houses. A lady was in her front yard pulling weeds. She smiled at him. *Do you know me? Do you know Casey?* He waited but she went back to her gardening. Kids whizzed by on bicycles. Dylan stopped. *Do you know me? Are you friends with Casey?*

It's hot out here. Dylan stayed on the sidewalk until he came to the corner. *There is a sidewalk on the other side, but I must cross the street to get to it. Casey said never to cross the street.*

Casey isn't here.

Dylan felt a wave of hot air. A small truck was parked at the curb with its engine running. Dylan recognized the big picture painted on its side. *That's a mail truck.* Joy sparked in Dylan's heart like mini firecrackers. *Claudia! She brings our mail to our house every day. Claudia can take me to Casey.*

He sniffed the open truck's door and looked inside. *No Claudia.* Dylan hopped inside anyway. *I can wait.* He kicked through some bundles of letters and magazines on the floor. When they fell out the open door on the other side, he settled himself down. *Much better.* Outside he heard quick steps coming his way. *Oh good. Here comes Claudia.*

A young woman climbed into the truck, reached for the gear shift, and screamed, "What are you doing here?"

Dylan's heart tumbled to his knees. *You're not Claudia.* He backed up as far as he could go. *Whine.*

"Shoo." She flicked her fingers in his direction several times. "Shoo."

Shoo? Dylan watched her fingers move back and forth. *Casey hasn't taught me that command.*

She got out of the truck, looked up and down the street, and then climbed back in. "Are you lost?"

Arf!

"Great, just my luck." She sighed, crossed her arms on the steering wheel and laid her head down. "What am I supposed to do with a lost dog?"

Whine. Take me to Casey.

She straightened up and glanced at her watch. "I should call this in but there'd be all kinds of paperwork to do. I'm already late." She pulled away from the curb. "You can stay lost until the end of my shift. Not my problem."

Dylan settled down on the floor of the truck. Whenever she stopped in front of a house to deliver the mail, he stuck his head out the open door. *Am I home?*

She drove for a while. Dylan felt the truck slow and

start to turn left. *No! You must stay on this street. That's where the Brea Country Club is.* The truck picked up speed. Looking out the open doorway on his side, Dylan saw the black asphalt of the street. *No! You're going the wrong way.*

I need to go home. Dylan closed his eyes and jumped. His shoulder hit the street hard. He tumbled over and over, paws and legs flying out. A blur of tires shot past him.

Screech!

Dylan curled himself into a ball.

Crash!

Thick, ugly scents filled the air, making Dylan's eyes water. Underneath him, the street was burning hot. He dragged himself up and into a sitting position. He saw a car resting on the curb. The front of the car had center-punched a streetlight. Steam rose from the car, sending up hissing smoke signals. An angry man slammed out of the car and raced toward him. "You stupid mutt! Look what you did to my car!"

Not me. Dylan shook his head and the dumb hair clip hit him in the eyes.

"Wait 'til I get my hands on you!" The man lunged for him.

Dylan ran.

The man's long legs ate up the space between them, coming closer and closer. Dylan could hear him breathing hard.

Dylan ran faster. He cut across a parking lot loaded with cars and looked for a way to escape the man.

Up ahead, a lady sat under an umbrella at a long picnic table. In front of her was a big sign decorated with balloons. Her face was raised to the stingy breeze, and she was fanning herself with a magazine. Beyond her, small tables were arranged under pop-up tents. People were milling about, going from tent to tent. Food scents told him he was hungry. People carried shopping bags. Music came from somewhere.

Dylan got excited. *I know this place! It's Farmers Market and I've been here lots of times with Mom. She buys stuff for dinner here. Next door is the Brea Community Center where Casey goes swimming. Maybe Mom and Casey are here.*

Dylan detoured toward the woman sitting under the umbrella. She didn't see him coming and he scooted under her table and out the other side.

The man's chase didn't let up. He ignored the woman and ran toward the entrance.

"Hold it right there." She tapped the sign in front of her with the magazine. "Admission is five dollars."

He whirled around. "Forget it, lady. I'm not buying anything."

Dylan padded over to a group of shady trees and collapsed on the ground. *That man is mad.*

The man put a scowl on his face and a hand over his heaving chest. "I'm chasing that stupid dog that ran out and wrecked my new BMW. I saw him come in here."

"I've been sitting here all afternoon and no dog has come in here."

"That's because you're blind as a bat and wouldn't know a dog if it bit you." He came closer to the table. "When I get ahold of that worthless mutt, I'm going to wring his pathetic neck."

The six-foot-two-inch woman stood up and straightened her Dylan's Dog Squad T-shirt. "No, you're not." She leaned on the table and pointed her index finger at him. "I'm going to tell you this one time and one time only. Get out!"

"No way." The man leaned on the table and got in her face. "You can't make me leave. The dog that wrecked my car is in there. I'm going to get him and he's going to be sorry when I do."

Oh-oh. Dylan remembered jumping from the mail truck and the car that almost hit him. *The broken car on the sidewalk must be yours. That's why you started chasing me.* Dylan scooted his buns farther back into the shade.

The man pushed away from the table, shook his fist at the woman and moved toward the entrance.

Not a wise move.

She blocked his way. "Security," she growled over her shoulder, "we have a situation here."

A man and woman security team came out of nowhere. The security woman spoke first. "Let's see some ID."

The angry man shot his fists into the air. "My ID is in my car." He ran his fingers through his hair. "I'm chasing a small, blond dog. He wrecked my car."

"Uh-huh," the security team said together.

"Sir," the security man said, "I'm going to ask you to leave quietly."

"Oh yeah? Make me." The man sneered and took a step closer. "I'm not going anywhere until I get my hands on that mutt."

"Call it in," the security man said to his partner. "Sir, you're coming with us."

"What for?" the man demanded.

"For being a troublemaker." The security woman turned away and clicked a button on her vest. "We're coming in."

"This is stupid. You're stupid," the man protested. "I'm not the one who caused the trouble. I'm telling you it's a dumb dog."

The security team each took an arm and started walking.

I need to stay here, out of sight. If anybody finds me, I'll be in trouble for breaking his car. They'll take me away, just like they took the man away. I'll never see Casey again.

NINETEEN

Mom stood back and held the door to the Brea Police Station open for Casey and Sumo. "Go ahead."

Casey and Sumo slipped past her.

Cadet Chen motioned them over to the reception counter. "Hi, Ms. Donovan. Hi, guys." She pressed a button and picked up the handset. "Captain Rizzoli, Ms. Donovan, Casey, and Sumo are here." She listened and disconnected. "The Captain will be right out."

"Thanks, Lisa."

Cadet Chen leaned forward on her elbows. "Everybody here is rooting for Dylan." Her dark eyes misted. "He's such a sweet little dog." She plucked a tissue from its box. "We can't believe he's disappeared, Ms. Donovan."

"We don't get it, either. Sumo, Casey, and Dylan's Dog Squad have been combing the neighborhood. No one has reported seeing him."

"What's weird," Casey broke in, "is that Dylan's famous. Thousands follow him on social media. He gets more attention than the President of the United States."

Captain Rizzoli's door opened. "Colleen. Boys." She hesitated. "We've got something to show you."

"What?" Casey clutched his Mom's arm.

"Has Dylan been spotted?" Sumo had his cell phone out and his fingers were tapping on the screen.

Captain Rizzoli gave a slight shake of her head. "It may be nothing. Cadet Chen, tell Lieutenant Kellan we're on our way back. Follow me."

They walked by the Report Writing Room. Officers glanced their way. Some waved. Some gave grim smiles.

Sergeant Yelin looked up from the paperwork on his desk and got to his feet. "Colleen. Boys. I asked the Captain if I could join you. I responded to the call earlier today."

Mom's voice dropped an octave. "What call?"

"Mom?" Casey's voice went small.

"In here." Captain Rizzoli opened the door to the Watch Commander's office. "Lieutenant."

Rory turned away from the monitors that lined one wall. "Hi, Sis." He came over and kissed her cheek. He nodded to Casey and Sumo. "This may be nothing, so don't get your hopes up."

Rory went to a computer and tapped a few keys. "Look at monitor number six."

"Is that Farmers Market?" Casey stepped closer to the screen.

"The call came in at two fifty-six today," Sergeant Yelin began. "Mrs. Langello was working Admissions."

"I know her," Mom said.

"Then you know she's a no-nonsense woman." Rory frowned slightly. "She reported a man causing a disturbance. When we responded to a call by security, the man, later identified as Robert Harris, told us he'd been chasing a dog. Harris claimed he was driving his new BMW at a safe speed on Birch Street."

Sumo snorted. "Don't all guilty people say stuff like that?"

"Anyway," Rory slanted his cop eyes Sumo's way, "a dog suddenly jumped out of a mail truck, causing Harris to lose control of his vehicle and crash into a streetlight."

"Was it Dylan?" Casey interrupted. "Is he hurt?"

"We don't know." Sergeant Yelin continued, "Harris said he then chased the dog into Farmers Market."

"Uncle Rory, what did Mr. Harris say about the dog?"

Rory hitched up his gun belt and moved away from his sister. "He said the dog was short, blond, fluffy, and ran like the wind."

"Dylan's not that short," Mom huffed.

"Yeah, he is." Casey's lower lip trembled. "He's just a little guy."

Rory turned to his sister. "Harris also said the dog was pretty and looked more like a stuffed animal."

"After we took Harris in," Sergeant Yelin cleared his throat, "I had a hunch the dog might be Dylan and ran the security tapes. This is what I found."

Rory pointed to another monitor. Curled up in the shadows of a tree was a little dog. His head rested on his front paws, but his face was turned away from the camera.

"Dylan!" Casey, Mom, and Sumo said together.

Casey pointed. "What's he wearing on his ear, Mom?"

"It looks like a little girl's hair clip."

Rory agreed. "Harris said he had ribbons on his ear."

"That doesn't make sense," Sumo argued. "Dylan was wearing his Dream Big bandana last night."

"True." Mom moved closer to the monitor. "Where's his collar? Do you have any more footage?"

"Sorry, Sis."

Her face fell. "If Dylan lost his collar, he's lost for sure. I'm sorry, Casey."

Casey shook his head. "Okay, that's bad but it's not so bad. Remember, Dylan's microchipped." He turned to Rory. "If someone finds Dylan, he'll take Dylan to the vet and we'll get called, right?"

Rory arched his eyebrows. "Let's hope so. Most people don't know pets can get chipped at eight weeks old. Most people don't do it even though it's easy. So," he let out a breath, "if they find a pet without a collar, they may not know to take it to the vet to see if it has been chipped."

Sumo raised his cell phone. "I just sent an update to Dylan's Dog Squad. I told them Dylan was spotted at Farmers Market, his collar is missing and," Sumo waved a hand in the air around his head, "he's got girly things in his hair."

"Thanks, Sumo."

"You bet, Ms. D."

Captain Rizzoli continued. "We contacted the Brea Post Office. A mail carrier named Fenton said she was driving her route. When she turned on Randolph Street, a very cute blond dog wearing ribbons on one ear jumped out of her truck and into the street. Fenton claims she didn't know the dog was in her truck. She also claims she didn't witness the accident between Harris's vehicle and the streetlight."

Sumo disagreed. "Like anyone could miss Dylan being in the truck. What's she hiding, Captain. Did you grill her?"

Captain Rizzoli gave a quick laugh. "Sorry to disappoint, Sumo. We don't grill people."

"That's a pity," Mom muttered. "Fenton just didn't want to be bothered reporting an accident."

Sergeant Yelin hooked his thumbs in his gun belt. "Neither her story nor Harris's story adds up, but no other witnesses have come forward."

"This is awesome." Casey broke into a big grin.

Everyone stared at Casey.

"Don't you get it, Uncle Rory? Mom? Randolph Street is near Farmers Market, so that means Dylan is in Brea."

Rory cocked his head. "What are you saying, Casey?"

"I'm saying, what are we waiting for? Let's go look for him."

TWENTY

Dylan's stomach growled. *I had one lousy Pop-Tart for breakfast and no lunch.* He heaved out a heavy sigh. *I wonder what Mom is making for dinner.*

Under the tree Dylan raked the leaves together with his front and back feet, plopped down, put his muzzle on his front paws, and worried. *If someone sees me, I'll get into trouble for breaking the man's car. If I stay here, I'll stay lost. I'll never see Casey or Mom again.* Dylan whined low. *What am I going to do?*

Small things rained down on Dylan's head, bounced off, and littered the ground around him. *What was that?* He shook his ears and crumbs flew out. He sniffed the crumbs. *Broken peanut butter cookies. Strange.*

"Hey, Dylan."

Dylan angled his face up. Dangling from a branch high above him were the bottoms of two sneakers. The small fist pelting him with cookie bits belonged to Jerome, the rude kid from the Read to Me Program. *What's he doing here?*

"Yeah, you," Jerome called. "Why are you by yourself?"

Jerome dove into the bag of cookies and shoved one into his mouth. "I bet that lamebrain Casey lost you."

Grr. Don't say mean things about Casey. Dylan's ears drooped. *I lost me.*

"Oh man," Jerome took a bite of cookie, "if you're lost, you're in *big* trouble." He chewed open-mouthed. "Animal Control will get called out here and a *big*, ugly, mean guy will grab you." He got up, spread his feet, and steadied himself on the limb. "Then the guy will throw you into a *dinky*, metal cage on a truck. Then you'll ride around in the truck *all* day getting hot and sweaty." He took another bite of cookie. "Just when you think you're done for," Jerome grabbed his throat with one hand and made gagging noises, "you'll get taken to the pound and thrown into a *big* cage with *big*, mean, nasty dogs."

Dylan blinked. *That doesn't seem fair.*

"After that," Jerome gave Dylan a sly look, "you don't want to know."

I know I don't want that. I want to go home to Casey.

Jerome turned chatty. "I'm supposed to be next door at the Brea Community Center taking dorky piano lessons." He waved a greasy, cookie-crumbed hand toward the white pop-up tents. "It's free babysitting while my mom goes to Farmers Market." He pointed to a backpack propped against the tree trunk. "My music is in there. She still hasn't figured out I've only learned one song."

I can't figure out why you're in a tree.

"As soon as Mom drops me off, I come over here. There are a zillion kids taking piano lessons at the Brea Community Center, so nobody misses me."

Nobody misses you because you're a rotten kid.

"I can see her from up here." Jerome made a grab for an overhead branch and missed. He wobbled a bit and put his arms out to steady himself. "When she finishes buying kale and whatever else she thinks is good for us, I climb down and head back to the Brea Community Center." Jerome laughed. "I've been doing this all summer."

You're weird.

Jerome dug another peanut butter cookie out of the bag. "Catch."

Dylan caught the cookie and chomped it down. *Thanks.*

"I wonder what yucky stuff she's buying today." Jerome put one hand on his hip and leaned forward. "Great. She's buying cauliflower. It makes the house stink like gym socks when she cooks it." He shifted and the branch underneath him dipped. "Hey, Dylan. Get my backpack and toss it up here. I want my water bottle."

You should come down.

Jerome wiped his grubby hand on his T-shirt. "Are you going to toss me the backpack or just stare at me?"

Dylan went to the backpack and used his teeth to try tossing it in the air. *Can't.*

"You're useless."

Am not.

"Casey's stupid to want a dumb dog like you." Jerome gave a little bounce. The branch groaned and sagged beneath him.

Grr. Dylan leaped up and planted both paws against the tree trunk. *Don't say mean things about Casey. If you want your dumb old backpack, come get it yourself. Grr.*

"You're growling at me? Like you're so tough." Jerome wadded up the cookie bag and pitched it at Dylan's head.

Crack!

The branch under Jerome's sneakers gave way. He grabbed for the overhead branch, missed, and tumbled down.

TWENTY-ONE

Dylan nudged Jerome's leg, but the boy lay still. Dylan's ears drooped. *You fell because I couldn't get your backpack. It's my fault you're hurt.* Dylan snuffled the boy's hand and face. *Please get up.*

Dylan sat back on his haunches. *I don't know what to do. I can't leave you, but I can't get help. If I go out there somebody will see me.*

Somebody will know it's my fault the car is broken.

Somebody will know it's my fault you're hurt.

Somebody will call Animal Control and they'll take me away.

I'll never see Casey or Mom again.

This is all my fault.

Fear pounded in Dylan's heart, making it hard for him to think. *I'm scared but I need to do something to help Jerome.* Dylan remembered the tall lady at the picnic table. *She stopped the angry man from chasing me. She called people and they took him away. She would know how to help Jerome.*

Dylan eased to his feet and searched the crowd at Farmers Market for the tall lady. He spotted her, still sitting at the picnic table, and still fanning herself with the magazine. *I'll get her to follow me to Jerome. She can call for help and I can run away.*

Dylan started walking but stopped. *What if she calls Animal Control instead? Then I'll never see Casey or Mom again.*

Jerome moaned and Dylan made up his mind. *Okay. Here goes. Be brave.* Dylan trotted out into the open, working his way through the shoppers, until he came to the tall woman. *Arf! Arf!*

She put her magazine down and cocked her head. "Are you the rascal that wrecked that man's car?"

Oh-oh. Dylan's courage poofed and his shoulders slumped. *Did you have to start with a hard question?*

She smiled and leaned forward to give him a scratch on his head. "I'm sure he deserved it. Dreadful man."

Really?

"Are you lost?"

Oh no. Another hard question. Maybe the tall lady wasn't such a good idea. He pawed her leg anyway.

"You must be thirsty." She took out a bottle of water from a cooler and filled a paper cup. "Here."

Dylan shoved his muzzle into the cup, sending the water up his nose. *Agh!* He tried again and this time he lapped the water until it was gone. *Thank you.*

"Hey! You're Dylan." She jumped up, pointed to his picture on her Dylan's Dog Squad T-shirt and then to Dylan. "Sumo has everybody looking for you."

Hooray! Dylan's heart floated like a fluffy cloud. *Everybody is looking for me! Thanks Sumo!* Dylan wiggled his whole body and the dumb hair clip hit him in the face. *Ow!* Dylan pawed at it.

"What's with the hair ribbons? You aren't a girl dog."

Tell that to Princess Amy.

"It must be pulling your hair. Let me take it off." She undid the clip and slipped it into her pocket.

Thank you.

She reached into her other pocket and took out her cell phone. "I'm texting Sumo to tell him you're here."

Yes! Dylan danced in a circle. *Casey and Mom will come get me. Yikes!* Dylan stopped dancing so quickly he tripped over his paws. *I forgot about Jerome.*

"What's the matter?"

Dylan jumped up, gently pounced on her knees, and ran a few steps toward the trees. He stopped and looked back over his shoulder. *Arf! Follow me.*

She studied the trees. "Is there something over there?"

Dylan scampered back to her and shifted his weight from one paw to the other. *Arf! Arf!*

"Okay, Dylan, okay. Carlotta," the tall woman called to a woman arranging a fruit display at a little table, "please watch Admissions for a few minutes."

Carlotta gave a half wave and went back to her work.

Dylan didn't wait for the tall woman but raced ahead to Jerome's side. *Help is coming.* Dylan belly-dropped to the ground, snuggled close to Jerome, and put his muzzle on his chest. *You're going to be okay.*

"Oh my," the tall woman gasped when she saw Jerome. "Good dog, Dylan." She knelt beside Jerome and listened to his chest. "He's still breathing. That's good." She took her cell phone out of her jeans pocket and pressed a button. "9-1-1? This is Maryella Langello at the Farmers Market. We have an emergency." The woman listened. "A small boy, maybe eight years old. He's unconscious." She looked around and saw the broken branch. "I think he fell out of a tree." She waited and smiled at Dylan. "Yes. One witness—Dylan, a very brave, smart dog."

TWENTY-TWO

A siren strained from far off, amped up and ended in a wail in the Farmers Market parking lot.

Maryella Langello turned her face in the direction of the sound. "That's the paramedics, Dylan." She was sitting on the ground by Jerome, holding his hand. "Now he'll get some help."

I don't know what paramedics are, but I'm glad they're here.

"Little boy," she squeezed Jerome's hand, "I wish I knew your name. I'd like to get a message to your parents." She studied Dylan. "Do you know who he is?"

I can't talk. Dylan whined and then dashed over to the tree and dragged Jerome's backpack to Maryella. *Maybe this can help.*

"Great idea, Dylan." Maryella gave the backpack a quick search and brought out a music book. "Oh, isn't this sweet. What a darling boy. He plays the piano."

Dylan's eyes flicked to Jerome. *More like one song.*

She opened the book to the first page. "His name is

Jerome Whitson. I'll give this to the police. Good job, Dylan."

Arf! Uncle Rory is the police. He'll know what to do.

Different sirens cut through the air, louder than the first. Dylan heard two whoops and then silence.

Maryella stood up and dusted the leaves from her jeans. "Sounds like the police just got here. It's going to get very busy. You need to stay close to me."

Dylan got excited. *I know lots of police officers.* He got to his feet and craned his neck, hoping to see his friends.

Instead of the police, two women in white shirts and dark pants hustled toward them, pushing something like a table on wheels. It bumped and bounced on the ground until they angled it close to Jerome.

"Paramedics," one woman announced, grabbing a bag off the table, and kneeling next to Jerome. "I'm Elizabeth and this is Hillary. Please stay back." She jutted her chin in Maryella's direction. "Are you the one who called this in? What can you tell me about the boy?"

"Not much except we have Dylan to thank for finding him. I was working Admissions. Dylan came to me and got me to follow him here." She gestured to a broken branch lying on the ground. "He must have fallen out of the tree. I called 9-1-1."

Dylan watched Elizabeth pull things from her bag. She put something with tubes in her ears and put something round on Jerome's chest.

Hillary pulled out her radio but pointed to Jerome's backpack. "Does that belong to the boy?"

"Dylan found it. I looked inside." Maryella handed the backpack to Hillary. "His name is Jerome Whitson."

"Thanks." Hillary turned away and spoke into the radio. When she finished, she said, "The police are out front, securing the area. I gave the boy's name to Sergeant Yelin. He's going to make an announcement over the loud-speaker. Hopefully his parents are here."

Dylan got excited. *I know Sergeant Yelin and he knows me. Whine.*

"Hey," Hillary said, looking from Maryella's Dylan's Dog Squad T-shirt to Dylan. "You're Dylan. Casey and Dylan's Dog Squad have been looking for you. Some kid named Sumo has been on social media, getting the word out that you're lost."

Dylan danced in circles. *Arf! Arf!*

Jerome moaned and rolled his head from side to side.

Hillary smiled at Dylan. "You woke him up."

Does that mean he'll get better?

"Stay still," Elizabeth put a hand on Jerome's shoulder, "you've had a bad fall. We're going to find your parents and we're going to get you some help." She started putting things back into her bag.

"Attention," a voice came over the loudspeaker, "will the parent or parents of Jerome Whitson please come to Admissions? Thank you."

Rory and two officers jogged in, saw them but veered in the direction of the paramedics without slowing down.

Arf! It's me!

"Be patient, Dylan," Maryella said, kneeling close and putting her hands on Dylan's shoulders. "Everybody has a job to do."

Rory spoke to Elizabeth, and then started walking over to them.

Dylan couldn't wait another minute. He broke free, ran toward Uncle Rory, and leaped up.

Rory caught him midair and hugged him. "Dylan!"

Dylan slurped doggie kisses over Uncle Rory's face. *You came! You found me!*

"Casey is waiting for you outside," Rory managed to say between kisses. "You had us so worried. Where have you been?"

I don't know but I'm glad you're here.

"Mrs. Langello? I'm Lieutenant Kellan. Dylan belongs to my nephew Casey." Rory dodged more kisses and shifted Dylan in his arms. "Thank you for contacting 9-1-1." He tipped his head toward Jerome. "He's starting to come around, but the paramedics think he has a concussion and a sprained wrist."

"The tree is old." She gestured to the broken branch on the ground. "Jerome's lucky. It could've been worse."

They watched while the paramedics lifted Jerome onto the gurney. Hillary set his backpack near his feet.

Chatter came from Rory's radio. He shifted Dylan again, turned away, and clicked the radio on. "Tell Mrs. Whitson they're bringing her son out now." He listened some more. "Yes, she can accompany him to the hospital." He turned back to them. "His mother's here."

Maryella sighed. "Thank heavens they found her."

They trailed behind the paramedics. The Farmers Market crowd had forgotten about shopping and stood around watching the paramedics lift Jerome and the gurney into the ambulance. An officer helped Jerome's mother climb inside and Elizabeth shut the door. Dylan leaned against Uncle Rory's shoulder. *I'm glad you found me.*

"Dylan!" Casey and Mom shouted.

Dylan swiveled his face around, keeping his muzzle on Uncle Rory's shoulder. His back paws kicked, and he squirmed to get down.

"Hold on, Dylan. You're going to fall."

Mom and Casey pushed through the crowd and wrapped their arms around Dylan and Rory.

Dylan poured on the canine kisses.

When Dylan squirmed some more, Rory handed him over to Casey. "Mrs. Langello, you know my sister Colleen Donovan, and this is my nephew Casey."

"Thank you, Mrs. Langello, for texting Sumo." Casey hugged Dylan tight. "You made my day. Right, Little Buddy?"

Right!

Maryella smiled. "Dylan is amazing. Not only did he take me to Jerome, but he brought Jerome's backpack to me. That's how I was able to learn his name." She reached out and stroked Dylan's ears.

"Dylan's really smart," Casey bragged. "Roger Bennett is his dog trainer. He's the guy who owns Dream Big K-9 Academy. He also trains police dogs and Search and Rescue dogs. Roger thinks Dylan could become a certified working dog." Casey frowned and added, "But I'm not sixteen."

Dylan sighed. *I'm not big like Dempsey and Joe Friday.*

"I know Roger," Maryella said. "He's always talking about his program. There are all kinds of certification. Roger must have something special in mind for Dylan."

TWENTY-THREE

In the hallway outside of Mom's office, Casey whispered, "Be quiet, Sumo. Mom is on Zoom with Cranky Pants."

"Don't let him see me," Sumo shot back. "I'm not posing for his stupid book again. That was so embarrassing. I had to wear a stupid bow tie and a stupid sweater that buttoned up in front like an old man's. I couldn't believe that wardrobe person found stupid wingtip shoes in my size. I looked like a total stupid geek. If any of the kids see the book, I'm dead."

"When it starts selling on Amazon, everybody will see it. You know it'll be a bestseller." Casey grinned wickedly. "Mom is getting the Brea Library to carry it. She's already made arrangements with our school library to carry a bunch of copies."

"I'm going to check out every book and lose them."

Casey tiptoed into Mom's office. Sumo tried hanging back in the doorway. Casey reached back, grabbed a fistful of Sumo's shirt, and dragged him in.

Hi guys. Dylan hooked his paws over the seat of Mom's big office chair and wiggled his buns.

Mom moved over a bit but kept talking. "I'm so glad you

like the illustrations Priscilla and Gina did for your book, Cranston." She shifted her eyes to Casey and Sumo.

Casey signed hi, by putting his hand to his forehead and drawing it away in a quick salute.

Mom faced her computer but angled the screen slightly away from Casey and Sumo.

Dylan watched Mom extend her index finger and pinkie finger on both hands and bring them together in Casey's direction. Dylan cocked his head toward Casey. *Why did Mom just sign hippo?*

Casey covered a big grin by biting his lower lip. Then he gave Mom a thumbs up. She beamed and went back to Cranston.

"Colleen the boy you found—Sterling—looks exactly like me when I was his age. We could be twins." His face crinkled into a happy smile. "The moment I saw him, I knew he was smart, sophisticated and will grow up to be just like me." He paused and looked skyward. "He is the hope of future generations."

Casey snorted and punched Sumo in the shoulder. "Sterling, the next generation. Sounds like the Star Wars television show."

Sumo stuck two fingers in his mouth and made gagging sounds.

"What's that noise, Colleen?" The old man's bald head swung left and right on his skinny neck, searching for the sound.

"Uh, owls." She sat up straight. "You know I live in a canyon. I have owls." Her eyes darted to Casey and Sumo. "Lots of owls."

"Owls only come out at night," Cranston argued.

"Uh, these are Brea city owls," she stammered.

"You just said you live in a canyon."

"Yes, the canyon—where I live is in Brea—the city."

Cranston scowled. "For heaven's sake, Colleen. Stop rambling and make sense."

Grr. Dylan leaned toward the computer. *Don't talk to Mom that way.*

Cranston brought his face closer to the monitor and warbled, "Is that Dylan? Such a precious little dog, just like my Scotch Tape. Dylan, do you want to visit your Uncle Cranston soon?"

Dylan shook his ears. *No way.*

Mom put one arm around Dylan and hugged him close. "He'd be delighted." Reaching for her cell phone, she found the calendar app. "Cranston let's get together next Tuesday to discuss marketing strategies. I can be in Beverly Hills at four o'clock."

"Fine."

She clicked End of Meeting, let out a breath, then sat back in her chair and swiveled. "Cranston's happy for the moment. What's up?"

"Not much. We're just hanging out."

"Can you do me a favor?" She shuffled through some papers on her desk. "I called Dream Big K-9 Academy and spoke to Jean. I told her Dylan lost his Dream Big bandana and chain collar with his identification tag."

Dylan looked down at his bare chest. *I'm naked.*

"Jean said she could replace all three." She found the papers she was looking for and held them up. "I'd go but I have to review these by three o'clock."

"Sure." Casey reached for Dylan and helped him out of the chair. "Ready for a road trip, Little Buddy?"

Arf!

"Oh, and Sumo," she smiled, "we got the invitation to

your mother's wedding. It was nice of her to invite Dylan, too."

Yay! I get to go to a wedding, whatever that is.

"I told her I wanted some of my friends there, too." He shrugged. "Mom likes Dylan."

She paused. "I understand her soon-to-be new husband owns a winery in Paso Robles. Will you be moving?"

"Nah," Sumo mumbled. "I've got school here and baseball in the spring. Mom says she'll travel back and forth." Sumo hitched a shoulder and let it fall. "When she's gone, Ingrid will take care of me. You know, like she always does."

Dylan rubbed against Sumo's leg. *Too bad you don't have a mom like our mom.*

"Mom, after Dylan gets his bandana and collar, can we get ice cream?"

Awesome idea, Casey.

"Sure, but only half a scoop of vanilla for Dylan."

Aw, Mom.

She glanced at Sumo. "Do you want to ask your mom if you can join us for dinner? We're barbecuing."

Yay! That means steak for me.

"We're also having corn on the cob, watermelon and strawberry shortcake."

Short cake? Dylan thought about that one. *I'm short. Must be a little cake. That's okay if I get some.*

Sumo perked up. "You bet. Thanks, Ms. D."

"Okay, Little Buddy. Time to hit the bricks."

Dylan zipped ahead of Casey and Sumo and raced down the stairs.

Before Casey opened the front door, he put a hand on Dylan's shoulders and held him back. "Just because you don't have a collar and can't walk on a leash, doesn't mean you can go crazy."

But I like it.

"You need to be careful."

All right, all right.

Casey let go. Dylan walked beside him to the bikes parked in the brick driveway. On a low wall a lizard sat swishing its tail. Dylan sniffed it once. The lizard did two pushups and then took off.

Sumo unhooked his bike helmet from the handlebars. "Your mom's so cool."

"Yeah, she's okay." Casey unzipped the bike trailer and helped Dylan into it.

"No, really. She's cool."

Dylan turned around in the bike trailer and peeked out the front at Sumo. *Too bad you can't live with us.*

"Move your face, Dylan." Casey waited for Dylan to back up and then zipped the front screen of the trailer closed. "Are you worried about your mom getting married again?"

"No way." Sumo laughed and hopped onto his bike. "She never stays married for long."

Ouch!

"The good news is this time I'm too old to be the ring-bearer." He put on his bike helmet and hooked the strap. "Wearing a tux really sucks."

Casey got on his bike, and they started riding to Dream Big K-9 Academy. Dylan put his snout next to the screen and sniffed as they raced along. *I'm a lucky pup. Riding in the bike trailer is the best.* Warm summer breezes sent smells his way. *Lots of things for me to see.* He settled down on his comfy cushion. *I have just enough time for a world-class snooze.*

When they turned into Dream Big K-9 Academy's driveway, Dylan shoved his face close to the side screen and looked out. German Shepherds, Great Danes, Mastiffs, Labradors, American Bulldogs and Golden Retrievers were running and playing games in the exercise field. Some were walking on the balance beams. He danced his four paws on his cushion. *I can do everything the big dogs can do.*

A Labrador was perched on top of the slide and looking at the girl waiting for him at the bottom. "C'mon, Jackson," she called. "You've got this."

Dylan held his breath for the big dog. *The first time I tried the slide, I was scared. Now I know it's fun.*

Jackson wasn't so sure. The Labrador put out a front paw and then took it back. He whined at the girl and started to pant.

"I'm right here, Jackson." She held her arms open to him.

This time he stepped out with both paws. She waved to him, and he lost his balance. The rest of him slid down the slide and his big buns plopped on the ground.

"Good dog, Jackson!" The girl flung her arms around his neck and squeezed.

Yay, Jackson!

"We'll park over here and check in at the office." Casey slowed his bike and stopped in front of the bike rack. He got off, put his backpack on the ground, and unzipped the front screen on the bike trailer.

Dylan stepped out into the sunshine. He stretched out his front and back legs, sniffed around and waited for Casey to sling his backpack over his shoulder.

"Okay, Little Buddy. Let's go see Jean."

Dylan forgot about being careful and raced through the open office door. He skidded to a stop at Jean's desk and pawed the lower drawer. *Arf!*

"Are you begging for a treat?" Jean tried to look mad but

couldn't pull it off. She opened the drawer, brought out the treat jar and held one out.

Dylan took it from her fingers and chewed with his mouth open. *Crunchy.*

"I've never known an American Cocker Spaniel to have such an amazing nose." Jean patted Dylan's head and put the jar of treats away. "It doesn't matter what drawer I have the treats in, he always finds them."

"Dylan can find anything," Sumo said.

"True." She brushed the crumbs from her hands.

Dylan agreed, sniffed the drawer, and looked back to Jean. *Seconds?*

"Nice try, Dylan. I have your things right here." She swiveled in her chair and took the Dream Big bandana and chain link collar from the credenza beside her. She swiveled back. "The collar is a medium. Dylan, sit."

Dylan sat and waited while she slipped it over his head.

Jean turned Dylan around and showed Casey the identification tag. "This has your contact information, but you'll have to order a new tag with his microchip information."

"Okay."

She smoothed Dylan's ears. "Hold still." She tied the bandana around his neck and smiled. "Very spiffy."

"Look over here, Dylan," Sumo said.

Dylan shook his head, making his collar jingle. Then he looked down at his new bandana and gave a tongue-hanging-out-of-his-mouth grin to everybody. *I'm no longer naked. I feel better now about the whole thing.*

Sumo took a picture and then his fingers went to work on his cell phone. "Let's show your public the latest."

"Thanks, Jean." Casey took Dylan's leash out of his shorts pocket and hooked it onto Dylan's collar. "Ready to get ice cream?"

Arf!

"Actually," Jean checked the time, "we have the American Kennel Club Canine Good Citizen class orientation starting in a few minutes. It's in the clubhouse. I told Roger you were coming today. He thinks Dylan would be a perfect candidate for the class."

"What's it about?" Sumo's fingers were ready to attack his cell phone.

"The AKC certification is a really big deal for a dog to get. All service dogs, therapy dogs, or emotional support dogs go through the training. If Dylan makes it, he'll get a patch to put on his vest."

Dylan's head popped up. The new bandana forgotten. *I've always wanted a vest. Dempsey has one.*

"The orientation will only take fifteen minutes. If you're interested," she took a pamphlet from a stack on her desk and handed it to Casey, "the application is inside. Talk to your mom and then let Roger know."

"What do you say, Little Buddy," Casey gave his leash a little shake. "Want to take another class?"

Dylan pranced in place. *I want a vest.*

"Okay, Jean. Thanks."

They walked across the parking lot and over to the clubhouse. Inside a Great Dane, German Shepherd, and Mastiff were seated at their owners' feet. Roger was talking to a woman with a Collie. He saw them come in and scowled.

"That guy's a real grump with people," Sumo said. "Good thing he works with dogs."

Casey snickered. "Have you ever noticed his arms and legs? They're always covered in Band-Aids."

They found seats in the second row. Dylan hunkered down next to Casey's feet and checked out the other dogs. *No vests.*

Sumo nudged Casey. "Are you sure we're in the right class? These are really big dogs."

I'm always the little guy. Sigh.

"Dylan can do anything those big dogs can do." Casey stroked Dylan's head. "Right, Little Buddy?"

Roger moved to the center of the room. "All right. Let's get started." He raised the American Kennel Club pamphlet. "The AKC Canine Good Citizen certification is for owners and dogs that share a special bond."

"Piece of cake," Sumo whispered. "You two have this bonding thing wired."

"Not every dog will get the AKC certification." Roger jabbed his iPad toward the audience. "Not the dog's fault. It's always the owner's fault. Owners are hard to train."

"Wow," Sumo rolled his eyes, "most people start by thanking people for coming."

Casey was flipping through the pamphlet. He stopped and showed a page to Sumo. "There are ten parts to the test. Looks like each one is a different skill."

Sumo got closer and read the list. "None of this looks hard."

Dylan rotated his buns and put his muzzle on Casey's knee. *What does the vest look like?*

Casey turned the page.

"Oh-oh," Casey and Sumo said together and slid their eyes to Dylan.

What?

"I'm not telling him." Sumo straightened up and sat back in his chair.

What? Dylan got up on his hind legs, pawed the book, and angled his head for a look. *Is this about the vest?*

"This may not be as easy as it sounds." Casey pulled

Dylan onto his lap. "You have only one chance to do each part of the test."

So?

"You have to do each part perfectly and on the first try."

Dylan flicked his ear. *All right.*

Casey made a face. "You can't have any treats when you're taking the test."

Grr!

Roger scowled. "Casey, do you have a question?"

Arf! I do!

TWENTY-FOUR

Casey held out Dylan's application for the AKC Canine Good Citizen class. "I called my mom and she said it's okay."

Roger snatched the application from Casey's hand. "What makes you think you can do this?"

"Dylan can do anything."

Dylan wiggled happily. *Anything to get a vest.*

"I didn't ask if Dylan could do this," Roger corrected, putting his hands on his hips. "I asked what made *you* think you could."

"If you didn't think we could do this," Casey shot back, "you wouldn't have told me about the class."

"Oh, for cryin' out loud—a kid philosopher." Roger glared down at Casey. "Save it for when you're thirty and in therapy."

"Have you always been this grouchy," Sumo interrupted. "Do you hate people?"

"Yes."

Whoa.

Casey and Sumo took a step back.

"Eight years I worked with people," Roger ran a scarred hand over his crew cut, "and I hated every miserable minute of it. All day long I'd hear them complain, complain, complain. Always about the dumbest things. Dogs are much better."

"Wow. That sounds awful," Casey agreed. "What did you used to do?"

"I was a doctor."

"Like a human people doctor?" Sumo crowed and clapped his hands together. "Get out!"

"Yup. That's what I did, kid." Roger pointed his iPad at him. "I cashed in my retirement, sold my six-thou-sand-square-foot home, and started Dream Big K-9 Academy." Roger rolled his shoulders back. "Best thing I ever did."

Good for you. Dylan looked at Roger's grass-stained shorts, ripped T-shirt, and grubby sneakers. *Where is your vest?*

Casey held up the pamphlet. "We'll start working on the test. See you in class."

Dylan pawed Casey's leg. *You're forgetting something.*

"You're right, Little Buddy. Let's celebrate with ice cream."

Yay! Dylan tugged on his leash, but Casey stood still. *Oh yeah. No tugging.* Dylan moved to Casey's left side, and they started walking.

"That blows me away," Sumo said as they crossed the parking lot to their bikes. "Why would Roger ever think he wanted to be a doctor?"

"Crazy, huh?" Casey unzipped the screen on Dylan's trailer and waited for him to get in. "Do you ever think about what you want to be?"

"You mean like when I grow up?" Sumo smirked. "I

don't have to be anything. My family's rich. What about you?"

"I kind of want to do what Roger does."

Dylan turned around and poked his nose out of the trailer. *Awesome.*

"You're kidding, right?" Sumo swung a leg over his bike.

Red shot across Casey's face. "I'm serious." He shrugged. "I never thought about being a dog trainer until I got Dylan. Now I think about it all the time." He ruffled Dylan's ears and then zipped up the screen. "It'd be fun."

We'd always be together.

"The catch is telling Mom." Casey shifted his backpack, swung his leg over, and reached for the handlebars. "She has this thing about me going to college."

"You could do both."

"You don't get it." Casey shook his head. "Being a dog trainer isn't exactly a professional job. You know how she is about books and stuff."

"Don't sweat it. Your mom's cool."

On the way to Brea's Ice Cream, Dylan thought hard. *If Casey wants to be a dog trainer, then I must pass the AKC Canine Good Citizen test. That would make Casey happy.* He wiggled his buns on his cushion. *When I pass, I'll get a vest and that will make me happy.*

Casey and Sumo parked their bikes and Sumo waited while Casey got Dylan out of the bike trailer.

Sumo rubbed his stomach. "I'm starving."

Casey looked around the patio outside Brea's Ice Cream. "Nobody is here."

"Is it closed?"

"I hope not."

Me, too. Mom said I could have vanilla ice cream.

They picked out a table. Casey got Dylan's blanket out

of his backpack and spread it smooth on the ground next to his chair.

Dylan claimed the blanket, kicked it into a heap with his front and back paws, and collapsed on it.

"Dylan!" Casey laughed.

Dylan looked up at Casey. *What?*

"I just fixed your blanket for you."

It's more comfy this way.

The doors of Brea's Ice Cream opened, and Crystal and Dominick came over to their table.

Dylan sat up and studied Crystal's and Dominick's plaid vests. *Have you passed the AKC Canine Good Citizen test?*

Crystal tapped Casey on the shoulder. "Look who's here."

"Exactly." Casey scooted his chair over to make room for her. "Where is everybody?"

"We were really busy after the ice cream stampede—thanks to Sumo and Dylan—but we've been dead ever since," Dominick said.

Crystal made a face. "Our corporate office is on my case about profits. I'm doing the best I can."

"You should talk to my mom. She's good at publicity. Look how the book launch for *Hieronymus the Hamster Goes to Nasa* turned out."

"That's true," Crystal mused. "I'll definitely call her. In the meantime," she elbowed Dominick in the ribs, "we have Dominick. He's our employee of the month."

Dominick rolled his eyes. "Big wow."

"What do you think," she pointed to the large cardboard sandwich sign near the entrance of the store.

FREE
ICE CREM PHOTO
WITH DOMINICK

"I haven't had my picture taken this many times since I was a baby," he grumbled. "Old ladies think I'm cute."

"Cheer up," Crystal laughed, "or I'll make you work overtime."

"I've got to get back to work, guys." Dominick gave Crystal a playful tap on the arm. "My manager is really mean. Bye, Dylan."

Crystal brought out her notepad and clicked her pen open. "What'll it be? Your ice cream is on the house for all the publicity you brought to us."

Ice cream on the house? I want mine in a junior cup.

"Dylan will have half a scoop of vanilla in a junior cup. I'll have a scoop of chocolate chip in a cup. Thanks."

"What about you, Sumo?"

"Mango sherbet and chocolate peanut butter with," he thought for a moment, "raspberry sauce, Oreo crumbles, walnuts and sprinkles."

Crystal's pen stay poised in the air. "Is that all?"

Sumo nodded. "I'm saving myself for strawberry short-cake at Casey's tonight."

"A wise decision," Crystal agreed. "Be right back."

"I'm telling Dylan's Dog Squad about the AKC Canine Good Citizen class." Sumo had his cell phone out and was working the screen. "This is a big day for Dylan. Pick him up and I'll take your picture, so I can send it out to all the social media sites."

Casey scooped Dylan up. "How about over here?"

"Too much sun." Sumo was looking at his cell phone and waving to his left. "Over there."

"Here?"

"Yeah." Sumo checked the picture and sent it out. "Just in time. Here's Crystal."

Casey put Dylan on his blanket, but Dylan immediately hopped up and put his paws on the table.

"Nice try," Casey gently pushed his paws away. "I'm pretty sure 'No eating with your paws on the table' is one of the ten tests you have to pass to get your vest."

Dylan slid to the ground. *Not fair.*

"Okay, guys." Crystal set her tray on the table and passed out the ice cream.

"Thanks, Crystal." Casey held Dylan's cup out to him. "What do you say?"

Arf!

"You're welcome."

Sumo was already shoveling ice cream into his mouth. He waved his spoon. "Thanks, Crystal."

"Looks like we might be getting some customers." She smiled, eying the parking lot as three cars drove in. "Enjoy, guys. Catch you later."

"Hold still, Little Buddy." Casey tried wiping Dylan's muzzle with a napkin, but Dylan jerked away. "I feel kind of bad Crystal gave us the ice cream for free. I had no idea the place wasn't making money."

"Yeah, I was thinking about that, too." Sumo's cell phone started vibrating and he picked it up. "Hey, we've got Dylan sightings here at Brea's Ice Cream." He put his cell phone down and dug into his ice cream. "Maybe that will help."

Screech!

Casey, Dylan, and Sumo looked over and saw cars, SUVs, and trucks pulling into the parking lot.

Dylan licked a little ice cream off his nose. *Good thing I already have mine.*

Car doors slammed and feet raced toward the ice cream shop.

Casey wiped his lips with the back of his hand. "What's going on?"

Sumo picked an Oreo crumble out of his ice cream mess. "Don't know."

"Oh, no. Wait a minute." Casey grabbed Sumo's cell phone and started scrolling across the screen. "Sumo!"

"Huh?"

Casey held Dylan's and his photo up. "Look!"

Sumo glanced over and mumbled through a mouthful. "Yeah, lighting wasn't the best but," he stopped chewing. "Oh man."

Dylan stood on his hind legs, put his paws on the table, and tipped his head to look at the screen. *What?*

"You moron! Look! Dylan and I are covering up 'Photo' and 'Dominick'".

FREE
ICE CREAM
WITH

Sumo's cell phone started dancing on the table. Two Brea Police cars zoomed into the parking lot, and Crystal was charging out the door, heading to their table.

Casey's cell phone went off. He dragged it out of his pocket, looked at the screen and held it up to Sumo. "Mom."

Oh-oh. Dylan dropped down on his buns. *You've done it again.*

TWENTY-FIVE

"Well, well, well." Captain Rizzoli swiveled in her chair and started with Mom. "The four of you are beginning to be a familiar sight in my office."

Mom smiled brightly. "Always a pleasure to see you, Captain."

Captain Rizzoli rolled her eyes. "Casey, Dylan, and Sumo, let me get this straight. In less than one week," she held up her index finger, "you have managed to cause two" she added another digit, "riots at Brea's Ice Cream."

What's a riot?

Captain Rizzoli focused on Mom. "This resulted in two of my patrol cars being dispatched to work crowd control." She shifted her cop eyes to Casey, Dylan, and Sumo. "Boys, what do you have to say for yourselves?"

Dylan sat up straight in his chair. *Their ice cream is really yummy.*

"We didn't think--" began Casey.

"Precisely." Her mouth flatlined. "You didn't think to bring me any ice cream."

Arf! Captain Rizzoli was making some excellent points.

"What's your favorite flavor," Sumo asked.

Captain Rizzoli slapped both hands on her desk. "Ugh!" When she looked at them again, she was slightly smiling. "What is it about the three of you? I have a hard time staying mad at you."

"Actually," Mom offered, "these minor incidences have helped Brea's Ice Cream. Because of Casey, Sumo and Dylan, they had a profitable afternoon."

Captain Rizzoli nodded. "Their business is struggling. Unfortunately, their location isn't the best for attracting customers. They really need some marketing gimmick to boost their profits."

Casey turned in his chair. "Mom, can't you do something? I told Crystal to call you. You're good at this stuff."

Sumo waved his cell phone in the air. "I can put the word out on social media."

"No!" they all chorused.

"Look, boys," Captain Rizzoli continued, "I'm glad you brought them some business today. The problem is when my officers responded, you used my resources. What if there had been an emergency and they were needed elsewhere?"

"I'm sorry," Casey mumbled. "We were celebrating. Dylan is starting the American Kennel Club Canine Good Citizen class soon. I want to get him certified, so we can do more things together."

I want to get a vest.

"Good for you, Dylan." Captain Rizzoli beamed at him. "You already do so much social work—the Read to Me Program and visiting at Children's Hospital. The AKC Canine Good Citizen certification is a natural fit."

Dylan gave her a happy grin. *Thanks, Captain.*

"Going back to the situation at hand," Mom prompted,

"there must be something we can do to help Brea's Ice Cream. We don't want them to close."

No way!

"Excuse me, Captain Rizzoli," Cadet Chen said as she knocked on the door jamb. "Hi everybody. Hi Dylan. How's Brea's favorite celebrity?"

Arf! Dylan liked Cadet Chen. She was cute and always had treats for him at the front desk.

Captain Rizzoli motioned her in. "Have things calmed down at Brea's Ice Cream?"

"So-so." Cadet Chen handed Captain Rizzoli a message slip and then stood behind her chair. She waited for the Captain to start reading the message before she gave everybody a wink.

"Are they serious?" Captain Rizzoli stared at Cadet Chen.

"Yes, Ma'am."

Captain Rizzoli waved the slip toward Casey and Dylan. "Brea's Ice Cream's corporate office is requesting Dylan's contact information."

Casey grabbed Dylan close. "They can't blame him for this. It's our fault."

"That's right." Sumo grabbed Dylan away from Casey and pulled him close. "We messed up. Make us wear their dorky old vests and scoop ice cream but don't take it out on Dylan."

You get to wear a vest? Dylan swiveled his head from Sumo to Casey. *What about me?*

"Relax," Captain Rizzoli held up a hand, "it's not what you think. As I mentioned, Brea's Ice Cream has been in a financial slump, but they're willing to take a leap of faith and hire Dylan."

Dylan studied his front paws. *I can't scoop ice cream.*

Mom leaned closer. "What do they have in mind?"

"They want to use Dylan as a," Captain Rizzoli searched for the right word, "spokesperson for their store."

I can't talk.

"Go on," Mom prompted.

"They want Dylan to do promotional work as soon as next week. They're willing to pay."

Mom offered a thin smile. "You must spend money to make money."

"Who is she quoting now?" Sumo whispered.

"Plautus, a Roman playwright," Casey whispered back.

Mom continued, "Considering their circumstance, how much could they possibly pay?"

Captain Rizzoli handed the message slip to her.

Mom's eyebrows shot up. "That much!" She glanced at Casey. "This could pay your college tuition."

"Wait until you tell your mom you're not going to college," Sumo snickered.

Mom froze. "Casey, what is Sumo talking about?"

"Uh, he means I'm not going to college just yet."

Dylan flicked his ears. *I don't think so.*

Mom let that sink in before turning back to Captain Rizzoli. "I have some ideas I'd like to discuss with Brea's Ice Cream." She smiled and started talking faster. "We could combine efforts here. What if we had Hieronymus the Hamster paint Dylan's picture in front of their store?"

I don't want to be painted by that dumb hamster. Dylan pawed Casey's arm. *Save me.*

"Mom," Casey laughed, "you're always working on a new book."

Her eyes sparkled. "It's what I do." She gave a happy toss of her head. "Who could we get to be Hieronymus?

Next week is short notice. It's too late to get an actor." She tapped her fingers on the arm of her chair.

"Somebody local would be ideal," offered Captain Rizzoli.

"Definitely excellent publicity," Mom agreed.

"What about Dominick," Casey suggested. "He's a college kid and is always trying to make money."

"No," Mom murmured, "too tall. We need someone considerably shorter. Someone who can fit into a hamster costume. Hmm. There must be someone."

Arf! Dylan rubbed against Sumo's arm.

One-by-one, Captain Rizzoli, Mom, and Casey turned to Sumo.

Sumo looked up from his cell phone. "What?"

Casey laughed. "Hello, Hieronymus."

"Aw, man."

TWENTY-SIX

"You're pouting."

Am not.

Casey moved in front of Dylan, thrust his index and third finger in the air toward him, signing Watch.

Dylan swiveled his buns and looked away. *I can't see you.*

"Hey, I don't make the rules."

You're following them.

Casey stepped in front of Dylan and crouched down. "Look, the AKC Canine Good Citizen rules say you have to do these tests without getting any treats."

I say the AKC hates dogs.

"The more we practice without the treats, the easier it will be for you to do the tests without them." Casey patted Dylan on top of his head. "Tell you what. While we're waiting for Sumo to finish talking with his mom, let's pretend we're taking the tests. When we finish pretending, you can have some treats."

Hmm. Dylan turned his face away, flicked his right ear and came back to Casey. *How many?*

"Do you want the vest or not?'

All right, all right. Dylan turned around.

"There are ten tests." Casey pulled the pamphlet out of his pocket. "Let's take the tests in order. I'm guessing that's how we'll do them on test day." He flipped through the pamphlet. "First up: Accepting a friendly stranger." He looked down at Dylan. "We don't have a friendly stranger."

Now what?

Ingrid came into the dining room carrying a tray with two glasses of lemonade and a plate of cookies. "Sumo said he would be here in a few minutes. He and Ms. Modragon are discussing her wedding plans."

"Uh, Ingrid," Casey took the tray from her and put it on the dining room table, "Dylan and I are practicing for the AKC Canine Good Citizen test. Can you help us?"

"Sure." She wiped her hands on her apron. "What do I do?"

"One moment." Casey read to himself from the pamphlet and then looked up. "This says you, the friendly stranger, are to come up to me and say hello. Maybe shake my hand. Anyway, you're supposed to ignore Dylan."

That's rude.

Ingrid smiled. "I would never ignore Dylan but today I'll make an exception."

Whine.

Casey was still reading. "Then you and I are supposed to talk for a minute, still ignoring Dylan." Casey ran his hand down Dylan's back. "All this time, Little Buddy, you're supposed to be okay with this. You can't butt in or act weird or bark at Ingrid."

Dylan sat down on his rump. *I'd never do that. I like Ingrid. She's nice to me.*

Ingrid looked around. "I could come into the room again and over to you. Would that work?"

"Okay."

Casey and Dylan waited for Ingrid. "You can do this, Little Buddy."

Dylan sniffed the air. *I can do this for cookies.*

Ingrid walked over to them, held out her hand to Casey. "Good morning."

Casey shook her hand. "Hi, Ingrid. Um," after a moment, he managed, "why is Sumo with his mom?"

"Wedding plans." Ingrid gave a long sigh. "The big day will be here soon, and Ms. Modragon wants everything to be spectacular. She has chosen the east lawn for the ceremony because it has a magnificent view of the lake. A dozen white swans are coming for the event."

What are white swans?

"You're kidding. A dozen white swans?" Casey scrambled for something else to say. "Uh, I'm glad she's having it here. She invited Dylan."

When Dylan heard his name, he looked from Casey to Ingrid but kept his buns on the ground. *I'm still behaving myself.*

"Ms. Modragon likes Dylan very much." Ingrid waited.

Casey checked the pamphlet. "Okay, I think that's it." He reached down. "Good job, Little Buddy."

Ingrid winked at Dylan. "Happy to help. I need to get back to the kitchen." She pointed to the table. "I made butter cookies so Dylan could have some."

Thanks, Ingrid.

"Thanks, Ingrid."

"That's the stupidest thing I ever heard! I'm not doing it!" Sumo shouted from somewhere in the house.

"It's the least you could do for me." Ms. Modragon's voice went up a notch. "It's my wedding!"

"So what? You're always having a wedding!"

Casey, Dylan, and Ingrid glanced at each other.

"Oh-oh," was all Ingrid said.

"Don't you dare slam that door, Sterling Ulysses Modragon!"

Slam!

Ingrid forced a smile. "As I was saying, I'll be in the kitchen." She bent down and stroked Dylan's topknot out of his eyes. "You're going to ace the test."

Sumo came into the dining room. "Hi, guys." He tossed a look over his shoulder. "Sorry about that. Mom is driving everyone nuts. Thomas the gardener is threatening to quit, and he's worked here thirty years."

Casey reached for a cookie, broke it in fourths and gave some to Dylan. "Everything okay? What's going on?"

Sumo helped himself to a cookie and bit in. "It's the usual wedding crazies. She just gave me the pre-wedding speech. You know the one about how Marvin isn't going to take the place of my dad but is going to be a really good friend."

"I thought his name was Michael."

"Hmm." Sumo stopped chewing and pointed the rest of his cookie at Casey. "You're right. Anyway, the kicker is since I'm too old to be a ringbearer this time, Mom wants me to walk her down the aisle."

Your mom can't walk by herself?

"Oh man," Casey agreed, "that sucks."

"No joke." Sumo shoved the last of the cookie into his mouth. "I'm stuck wearing a stupid tux again, and it's peach. *Peach.*" He shuddered.

Peaches are yummy.

"I think she's had all the other colors already. Anyway," Sumo said again, "I've got to go by the tux place and get fitted. Can we do that before we go to Jake's?"

Can we finish the cookies first?

"Yeah. It's just a bunch of kids hanging out." Casey gave Dylan another piece of cookie. "Where is the place?"

Sumo brushed the crumbs from his hands and took a long drink of lemonade. "It's called Forever in Love. It's where she buys all her wedding dresses and stuff." He put down the glass. "Let's get this over with." Sumo snatched two more cookies. He tossed one to Dylan who caught it midair and gulped it down. "I'll go get my bike."

When they were outside, Casey and Dylan waited while Sumo went to the garage for his bike. Dylan sniffed around the bushes a bit and then lifted his muzzle to the sunshine.

After a while, Casey unzipped the front screen on the bike trailer. "Here you go." Dylan hopped in and turned around twice on his cushion. Casey knelt and fondled Dylan's ears. "I have a bad feeling about all this. What if Sumo's mom changes her mind and wants to move to Paso Robles? That's like five hours away."

That's too far to ride your bike.

"Mom says if you're not happy for your friends, you're being selfish." Casey took a deep breath. "I can't help it. I don't want Sumo to go. He's my best friend."

Dylan snuffled Casey's hand. *Mine, too.*

"Ready." Sumo skidded his bike to a stop in front of them. "Follow me."

Forever in Love was a short ride, but it gave Dylan time to think. *A wedding sounds like a big party. Parties are supposed to make people happy, but Sumo isn't happy.*

Dylan put his muzzle on his front paws. *Why did Ms. Modragon invite a dozen swans?*

As soon as they entered Forever in Love, an eager man in a grey, pinstriped suit rushed to greet them. "Welcome! Welcome!" He tried to grab both Sumo's hands, but Sumo danced back. "Sterling, so wonderful to see you again!"

"It hasn't been that long since Mom's last wedding, Mr. Franco." Sumo turned to Casey and snorted, "If Mom stops getting married, Forever in Love will have to rewrite their business plan."

"I'm Bernard Franco." Ten manicured fingers straightened a perfectly knotted silk tie. "I'm a dear, dear friend of Selena Modragon."

"Hi. I'm Casey and this is Dylan."

"Dylan!" Bernard crossed both hands over his heart and swooned.

Grr. Dylan scrambled behind Casey and peeked around his legs. *You're weird.*

"I follow Dylan on social media!" the man gushed. "I'm ecstatic to meet the little doggie that found the boy at the mall."

"Dylan can find anything or anyone. Right, Little Buddy?"

I like helping people. It makes me feel good.

"Sterling, I've personally laid your tuxedo out in the dressing room!" His slender hands clapped together. "We need to get you fitted! The big moment is only days away!"

"Thanks for reminding me," Sumo said dully.

Dylan pawed Casey's leg. *Weird Bernard is more excited about the wedding than Sumo is.*

Bernard Franco motioned them to follow. "It's been thrilling planning Selena's wedding. I love her theme— Southern Splendor. Her dress is an inspiration." He stopped and circled his hips with his hands. "Yards and yards of skirt."

"Southern? Like in *Gone With the Wind?*" Casey made a face. "We live in Southern California, not Georgia."

"I think Milton is originally from Georgia."

"Michael."

"Whatever."

"This dressing room is the size of my classroom at school," Casey whispered to Dylan when they followed Bernard inside. "Check this out. There's got to be ten mannequins in here. Talk about creepy." Casey pointed to a mannequin wearing a purple ruffled shirt. "I'm glad Sumo has to wear this stuff and not me."

Dylan studied the mannequins decked out in jackets, shirts, slacks, and shiny shoes. *That's a lot of clothes.* Then he studied Sumo's skinny arms and legs sticking out of a washed-out T-shirt and baggy shorts. *No wonder you're not excited.*

Without being told Sumo yanked the peach tux that was laid out on a table near the tri-fold mirror. Dragging it behind him on the floor, he disappeared into a dressing room to change. After a few minutes he came out and stood in the middle of the room with his hands out to his sides. "I look like a bottle of peach Snapple."

Casey tapped Dylan on his shoulder and put his index finger to his lips, signing Quiet.

That's too weird to bark at.

A young man with a tape measure and an iPad came into the dressing room. "Hi."

"This is Clifton, my assistant." Mr. Franco's cell phone chimed, and he checked the readout. "Ms. Modragon requires my attention. I shall return."

Clifton nodded and got to work.

Casey guided Dylan over to a pale pink velvet loveseat and helped him up. Dylan snuggled close to Casey and laid his muzzle across Casey's lap. Sumo held out one arm, then the other one and Clifton measured. Clifton dropped to one knee and measured Sumo's legs.

Dylan stretched out his front legs and studied them. *Mine are furry.*

"That's it," Clifton said after he made the last entry on the iPad. "Mr. Franco will call regarding a final fitting."

"Thanks."

Bernard bustled into the dressing room and held up his cell phone. "Ms. Modragon called with the most brilliant idea." He raised his eyes to the sparkling chandelier and crooned, "Only she would dream of having the famous Dylan as her ringbearer."

Huh?

"Imagine that!" he marched in place and beamed.

"Yeah, imagine that," Casey echoed. "Sumo?"

"News to me."

Dylan checked out the mannequins and gave a low whine. *No dog mannequins.*

"I've never dressed a doggie before," Bernard mused, putting a slim finger to his chin, and tapping it a few times. "But Bernard Franco is always up for a challenge!" Tap. Tap. Tap. "Ah, yes, I have the perfect idea for Dylan. One moment."

Sumo came over to Casey and Dylan. "Look, you're my best friends. You don't have to do this."

"What do you say, Little Buddy?"

I say we need to do this for Sumo. Arf!

"If Dylan is okay with it, I'm okay with it." Casey stroked Dylan's back. "Mom's going to love this."

Sumo shoved both hands into his pockets. "Thanks, guys."

Bernard beelined into the dressing room, holding something behind his back. "My expert eye tells me Dylan is a four."

I'm an American Cocker Spaniel.

"Voila!" With a flourish, Bernard whipped a peach silk vest out from behind his back and held it up. "Children's size four. Fabulous, yes?"

A vest! Wow! Not a dorky tux.

"No!" Sumo and Casey shrank back.

Why not?

"Time for your fitting, Dylan," Bernard announced and waved the vest toward Dylan.

Dylan hopped off the couch and stood still while Bernard slipped his left front leg into an armhole and then his right front leg into the other armhole.

"Please sit. We need to button the front."

Dylan sat.

Bernard's nimble fingers brought fabric and buttons together and then he tipped his head to admire his work. "A most excellent fit, if I do say so myself."

Dylan dropped his muzzle to his chest and checked himself out. *My first vest.* He rubbed his muzzle on his shoulder. *Soft.*

"Oh no, little doggie." Bernard's voice went soprano. "Silk is very sensitive. You mustn't do that. You will leave drooly marks on the fabric."

Sorry. Dylan looked up at Casey. *I've always dreamed of a vest.*

Casey gave a half laugh. "This isn't exactly an AKC Canine Good Citizen vest," he smiled, "but you do look sharp."

Sumo took a ringbearer's silk pillow from a display case. "How is Dylan going to hold onto the rings?"

Dylan shook out his front paws. *Oh yeah.*

"We will sew a tiny pocket here." Bernard's finger traced an area above Dylan's heart. "Perfect!"

TWENTY-SEVEN

Whoa. Dylan sat down hard on his rump.

"I had no idea the AKC Canine Good Citizen test was such a big deal." Casey bent down and rubbed Dylan's shoulders. "How many dogs are here?"

I can only count to three.

Casey put his hand up to shade his eyes from the sun. "There's got to be a zillion."

That's more than three.

The exercise field at Dream Big K-9 Academy was one big furry moving mass of canines. Some owners were calling commands to their dogs. Other owners moved with their dogs, doing training exercises. On the sidelines men and women wearing armbands and carrying iPads pointed to dogs and talked to each other.

A man walked by with a Giant Schnauzer wearing a vest with an AKC Canine Good Citizen patch. The man gave a friendly wave. "Good luck today."

"Thanks!" Casey bent down and tied Dylan's Dream Big bandana around his neck. "I saw you looking at that dog's vest."

Dylan peered over Casey's shoulder. *I'm still looking.*

"I bet all last night you were dreaming of getting your vest."

Was not. Dylan wiggled his buns. *Maybe just a little.*

Casey patted Dylan's bandana into place. "You'll have one, too. You've worked very hard, and you know your stuff." Casey kissed Dylan on top of his head. "After you pass the test, we're meeting Sumo, Jake, Tabitha, Tanya, and Tori for pizza at Big Belly's to celebrate."

Yes!

"Registration is now open for the ten o'clock group," a voice boomed over the intercom. "Please proceed to the registration desk."

"That's us." Casey stood up. "Let's go."

I really want this. Dylan stayed put. *But these dogs are huge.*

"Okay, so you're a little scared, but you're not alone. This is a big dream for every dog here. It's okay to be scared. If dreams were easy, they wouldn't be such a big deal. Think about all the things you learned in Agility class. Remember when you thought you couldn't do the balance beam?"

I fell off.

"Remember when you didn't want to go down the slide?"

I slipped and slid muzzle-first down the slide and hit my snout on the ground.

"Remember when you got lost in the tunnel?"

It was really dark in there. You came in and found me.

"And what happened?" Casey ran his hands over Dylan's ears and down his back. "You learned to do all those things. Now you do them for fun."

Dylan sat up straighter. *Just like the big dogs.*

"Don't be scared. I'm with you." Casey straightened Dylan's Dream Big bandana. "When we leave, you'll be wearing not only your bandana but a vest with an AKC Canine Good Citizen patch."

Dylan looked at his curly furry chest. *I've always wanted a vest.*

Casey brought out a Ziploc bag of treats from his shorts pocket and held one out. "How about a treat for good luck?"

Dylan chomped it open-mouthed. *I'm feeling better now about the whole thing.*

Casey slung his backpack over his shoulder, and they walked to the registration table.

"Hi, Mrs. Langello. I didn't know you'd be here today."

The tall woman stood up. "I help Roger out whenever I can. We've been friends for years."

Dylan rubbed against Casey. *Grumpy old Roger has friends?*

She came around the table and crouched down to pet Dylan. "I saw your names on the sign-up sheet. I was hoping I'd see you. We have quite the crowd today." She brushed a hand down Dylan's ear. "Is this his first time to take the AKC test?"

"Yes."

First time? Dylan got up on his hind legs and pawed Casey's thigh. *What does she mean?*

"It's okay. Don't worry." Casey scratched Dylan's neck and turned to Mrs. Langello. "Dylan's nervous. He's always the only little guy."

"Being a little dog is a good thing, Dylan."

No, it's not.

Casey said, "When you work at Children's Hospital,

you're small enough to fit into a wheelchair or lie on a hospital bed. The big dogs have to stay on the floor."

Oh yeah, serves them right!

"We've been practicing. Dylan knows he has to do the tests perfect and on the first try."

And without treats. Dylan sighed and slid down to the ground. *So unfair.*

"I know the rules seem hard, but sometimes hard only means you have to try harder." She straightened up. "When Dylan passes the test, he will have earned the AKC Canine Good Citizen patch. Only the best dogs get to wear it on a vest."

Dylan danced in place. *I can't wait for my vest.*

She handed Casey two papers. "This is the test. You know Jean." She pointed to the dark-haired woman on the exercise field. "You'll be working with her today. Good luck!"

"Thanks."

Dylan trudged alongside Casey and thought. *If I don't pass the test, I don't get a vest. If I don't pass the test, I'll let Casey down. Casey wants me to pass the test because he wants to be a dog trainer like Roger.*

I've got to pass the test.

"Hi, Casey." Jean smiled and tucked her iPad under her arm. "This is a big day for you, Dylan."

This is a lot of pressure.

"Ready? Let's get started. Test number one: Accepting a friendly stranger." Jean moved away from them.

"You've got this, Little Buddy."

Dylan sat. When Jean came up and shook Casey's hand, Dylan watched just in case she dropped a treat. *Nope.* After they talked for a minute, Jean left, and Dylan began to relax. *There's nothing to this.*

Jean came back. "Test number two: Sit politely for petting."

When Jean rubbed her hand over Dylan's shoulder, he stared up into her face. *You can pet me all day.* He shifted slightly so she could rub his other shoulder. *Ah, nice.*

"You're making my job easy," Jean said after she made a note on her iPad. "Test number three: Appearance and grooming. Casey, do you have his comb and brush?"

Casey got them out of his backpack and handed them over.

When Jean ran the brush down Dylan's back, he wiggled. *Tickles.*

"Okay, let's take a five-minute break. Give Dylan some water. I'll be back."

After Jean walked away, Casey got Dylan's collapsible cup out of his backpack and poured water from a bottle.

Dylan lapped it up and shook his muzzle. *This is going great.*

"I'm proud of you."

Thanks.

When Jean came back, she checked her iPad. "Test number four: Out for a walk on a loose leash." She motioned for Casey and Dylan to start walking. "I'm going to call directions out to you. When I say left, turn left. When I say right, turn right. Understand?"

"Dylan knows left and right in sign language, too."

Jean's eyebrows went up. "Very good."

"We're up to about fifty words and phrases."

Arf!

Casey and Dylan walked a bit. When she told them to turn right, they did.

"Stop."

Casey and Dylan stopped.

"Walk for ten feet and turn left."

They did.

"Okay, come back."

Dylan pranced alongside Casey. *How many more tests?*

"Follow me to the parking lot." Jean was already heading in that direction. "Test number five: Walking through a crowd."

Oh-oh. The parking lot was crowded with big dogs, handlers, and judges. Dylan moved closer to Casey. An Irish Setter bumped into Dylan. *Hey!*

A woman with a Great Dane turned in front of them. The Great Dane stopped, dropped its muzzle down to Dylan's face and panted. *You've got biscuit breath.* Dylan skirted around him and walked faster. *I hope this test is over soon.*

Dylan was busy dodging people and didn't see the kid on a skateboard. The kid whizzed by, clipping Dylan with the skateboard. Dylan whipped around and pounced. *Grr.*

"Hey," Casey shouted after the kid.

"Sorry, man." The kid gave a careless wave in the air and kept moving.

Casey dropped Dylan's leash, started after the kid, and yelled, "Get back here."

The kid faded into the crowd. Casey came back and grabbed Dylan close. "You're shaking. Are you hurt? I'm sorry, Little Buddy, I didn't see him."

Dylan turned his body into Casey's. *He scared me.*

Jean checked Dylan's paws. "I think he's all right. Just frightened."

"Who was that kid? Dylan could've been hurt."

Jean's mouth flatlined. "He was a planned distraction." She put her hand up when Casey started to protest. "Yes, he came too close, and I'll talk to him about it. Unfortunately," she slanted her eyes to Dylan, "the distraction worked."

Casey pulled Dylan closer to him. "What are you saying?"

"I'm sorry Casey. I'm saying Dylan flunked the test."

TWENTY-EIGHT

Dylan's spirit crumbled and his heart fell to his knees. *Say it isn't so.*

"This isn't right, Jean," Casey protested. "That kid could've hurt Dylan. Dylan was just defending himself."

Jean gave a small shake of her head. "I agree but I can't bend the rules for you. You know a dog is automatically disqualified if it snaps, bites or growls in a test situation."

I should've kept my grr to myself. Dylan hung his head. *I let Casey down. I feel smaller than a chihuahua.*

"I'm truly sorry." Jean checked her iPad and swiped across its screen. "We have another test scheduled in a few weeks. Dylan can try again."

"We'll think about it. Thanks, Jean." Casey gave Dylan another hug. "Let's go, Little Buddy."

Dylan plodded alongside Casey, trying to ignore the happy dogs and owners walking by. *All the dogs are wearing a vest with an AKC Canine Good Citizen patch except me. I'm a loser. Now Casey can never be a dog trainer and he'll have to go to college and read stuff.*

He hates reading.

He must be really mad at me.

When Casey reached his bike, he knelt and unzipped the front screen on Dylan's trailer.

Dylan brushed past him, anxious to get in. *I'm never coming out again.*

"Hold on." Casey grabbed Dylan by the shoulders, backed him out of the trailer and turned him around. "We need to talk." Casey sat on the ground and pulled Dylan onto his lap. "Let's get one thing straight."

Oh no. Here it comes. You're mad.

"I'm so sorry."

Huh?

"I know how much you wanted to pass the test." Using his index finger, he tipped Dylan's muzzle up, so Dylan had to look at him. "Okay," Casey gave a small laugh, "maybe it was really the vest."

Well, yeah.

"You're my Little Buddy."

Dylan searched Casey's face. *Are we okay?*

"Listen, I want what you want." He leaned closer, nose-to-nose with Dylan. "If you want to try again, we will."

You want to be a dog trainer. I want what you want.

Casey got up and put Dylan into the bike trailer. "Guess what?"

Dylan peeked out. *What?*

"It's time to meet the kids at Big Belly's for pizza."

Dylan cocked his head. *I didn't pass the test.*

Casey lifted his right hand, put up his little finger, his index finger and then his thumb.

Dylan gave Casey a tongue-hanging-out-his-mouth grin. *I love you, too.*

TWENTY-NINE

Sumo held a brown, gold, and white hamster head under his right arm and fisted a left paw on a furry hip. "It's not fair," he griped. "I have to wear this stupid hamster costume and this dorky plaid vest."

Dylan started with the pink feet of the Hieronymus the Hamster costume and rolled his eyes up to where Sumo's head was sticking out. *This is even weirder than those dumb hamster pictures.*

"It's not fair," Sumo repeated.

Sumo's right. It's not fair! Dylan whined low. *He gets to wear a Brea's Ice Cream vest and I don't.*

Casey busted up. "It's not so bad."

"Because you're not stuck wearing them." Sumo dropped-kicked the hamster head, and it rolled away.

Dylan scampered after the head and clamped his jaws on an ear. He shook the head back and forth and then spit it out. *Yuck. Kind of like a fuzzy ball.*

"Bring it here, Little Buddy." Casey clapped his hands together.

"I thought your mom liked me."

Dylan swiped at the hamster head with his left paw and then his right paw, chasing after it until it rolled back to Casey. *Hamster soccer!*

"She does." Casey snatched the hamster head up and tossed it to Sumo. "That's why we're doing the Brea's Ice Cream promo event today. She thought you'd be too busy with your mom's wedding after this."

"Nah, I just have to show up and walk Scarlet O'Hara down the aisle. Or try to. Her dress is as big as a circus tent. This whole *Gone With the Wind* theme is her stupidest wedding theme yet. If we get a big blast of wind, she'll be flying over Orange County and end up in the Pacific Ocean."

"It's really windy today." Casey straightened Dylan's bandana and smoothed his topknot down. "Dylan looks like Doc Brown from *Back to the Future.*"

That crazy old guy climbing the clocktower in the storm? Dylan shook his head, and his topknot sprang back up. *Not me.*

"The breeze feels good," Sumo grumbled pulling at the fur around his neck. "This costume is hot."

"Maybe we're getting a summer storm."

"Uh-uh. The wind is supposed to pick up but be gone by three o'clock."

Casey scowled. "How do you know this stuff? Have you been reading again?"

Sumo snorted. "Mom's going nuts about her outdoor wedding. She's glued to the weather channel. I get a weather update like every hour."

"Her wedding will be over soon."

"Yeah, I can't wait." Sumo covered his eyes with little, pink hamster paws. "What if the kids from school see me today in this getup? I thought dressing like Cranky Pants was bad enough. This is so humiliating."

"If you put the hamster head on, no one will recognize you."

Sumo angled into the hamster head. "What do you think?"

Whoa! Dylan stepped back. *A five-foot-tall Hieronymus. That's really scary.*

"Hi boys. Hi Dylan."

"Hi, Ms. D."

Dylan moseyed closer to Mom, sat down, leaned against her knee, and looked up. *Want some vanilla ice cream?*

"Hi, Mom."

She bent down and ruffled Dylan's ears. When she looked up, she studied Sumo and then fluffed out some fur around his shoulders. "You look adorable."

Sumo flicked a whisker with his paw. "I've always wanted to be a hamster, Ms. D."

Seriously? Dylan drew his head back for a better look. *You should change your mind.*

"I've got to get a picture of this." She held up her cell phone. "Say cheese."

"Aw, Ms. D," Sumo waved both paws in the air, "that's so corny."

The hamster head must be on too tight. Corn isn't cheese. Even a dumb hamster should know that.

Casey rubbed his hands together and a big grin shot across his face. "Almost show time. What are Sumo and Dylan doing today?"

The double doors to Brea's Ice Cream opened. Crystal and Dominick carried out a square table covered with a brown cloth. A giant wicker basket sat on top, filled with white, fluffy material. They put it in front of a backdrop of blue sky and fat white clouds. A big banner stretched across the backdrop. "Hieronymus the Hamster Paints Dylan! Get Your Free Autographed Poster Here."

Crystal and Dominick disappeared back inside the shop and a minute later came out with a huge stack of posters, a fistful of paintbrushes, and jars of red paint. Dominick dragged a long table over to the basket table and put the paint supplies on it. Crystal set the posters on the long table.

When they finished, Crystal turned around and called, "What do you think, Colleen?"

"It's great! Thanks so much!"

"What is all this stuff, Ms. D?"

She gestured to the display. "The wicker on the basket is like the design on Brea's Ice Cream dish. We fluffed up the white material inside the basket to look like three scoops of vanilla ice cream. Dylan will sit on the middle scoop of ice cream next to the round, red velvet pillow. That's the maraschino cherry. We scattered wood bark on the white material to look like nuts."

"So much for truth in advertising, Mom," Casey snorted.

"In this world, perfection is an illusion."

"Wow, Ms. D, that's interesting."

"That's Tite Kubo." Casey rolled his eyes. "He's a manga artist."

What's manga?

Mom ignored Casey. "I took pictures of the props, got pictures of Dylan and Hieronymus, and brought everything to Brea Office Supply. They created the posters of Hieronymus painting Dylan sitting in an ice cream dish."

I like ice cream for eating. Dylan shivered. *My buns wouldn't like it for sitting.*

"Now what, Ms. D?"

"When a customer comes out of Brea's Ice Cream, Hieronymus--that's you Sumo--will use the fast-drying poster paint to sign Hieronymus in the corner of the poster and give it to him."

Sumo had the hamster head off again and was twirling it around on his paw. "That doesn't sound too bad, Ms. D."

She arched her eyebrows and gave a thin smile. "It was the best idea I could come up with on such short notice. We had to move up this promo event because your mom moved up the wedding rehearsal to tomorrow night."

"Yeah, what's with that?" Casey interrupted. "The Padres are playing the Giants this afternoon. Jake was coming over with hot wings, barbecue potato chips, and Rice Krispy treats. We're going to miss the game."

And the junk food.

Sumo tossed the hamster head from paw to paw. "Mitchell has to leave right after the wedding rehearsal and drive to Paso Robles. Summer is bottling time at his winery. Something about he's got to get wine samples to the wine lab before his winery can bottle the wine. Tomorrow night is the only night Mitchell can be here for the wedding rehearsal. Sorry, Ms. D."

Her eyes flicked to Sumo. "Isn't his name Michael?"

"Whatever."

"Okay." Mom let it go. She took three bottles of water out of her purse and handed them over. "Here's some water in case you get thirsty. I have a meeting and will be back in two hours. If you need anything, text me or see Crystal." She checked her cell phone. "Time to start."

Casey jiggled Dylan's leash. "How long do Sumo and Dylan have to do this?"

"I've sent out several social media blasts. Brea Campers is bringing a bunch of kids. They have their choice of vanilla or chocolate ice cream, so it should go fast inside the store. I had a hundred posters printed. There will probably be a lot left over." She brushed her hair out of her eyes. "The wind is really picking up." She gave them a little wave. "See you soon."

Casey punched Sumo in the arm. "Show time, Hieronymus."

"Don't even think about leaving me." Sumo dropped the hamster head into place. "If I've got to be here, so do you."

"Hey, look! Jake, Tabitha, Tanya, and Tori showed up." Casey waved both hands high in the air. "Over here!"

"I'm warning you," Sumo hissed, "tell them it's me in this getup and you're dead."

"Aw, and you look so adorable, too." Casey laughed but jumped back when Sumo swung out with a pink paw. "C'mon, Little Buddy. Time to check out the basket. Hieronymus is getting grouchy."

Casey lifted Dylan up and settled him onto the white fluffy material.

Does it taste like ice cream? Dylan sniffed and gave the white stuff a few licks. *Nope.* He pranced back and forth on the material. *Bouncy!* He plunked his buns down. *Nice.* He wiggled his buns in a little circle. *Really nice.*

"Stay still." Casey fluffed the white material around Dylan. When he put the maraschino cherry pillow next to Dylan, it started to roll away. Casey caught the pillow, pushed it down hard in the material, but it bounced out of the basket. "Aw, forget it."

Dylan dropped to his stomach but got back up. *The wood bark is scratchy.* He kicked the pieces out of the basket, turned around once and stretched out. *Much better.*

"Hi, Casey and Dylan," Tanya, Tabitha and Tori called. They rushed forward, got their cell phones out and hip-bumped each other for a place around the big basket. Tossing back their long hair, they hunkered behind Dylan, and held their cell phones up for selfies. "Dylan, smile," they squealed. "Dylan, look!" They shoved their cell phones under Dylan's nose so he could see their pictures.

"I hate my hair!"

"I look fat!"

"You look cuter than me!"

Dylan slurped a kiss on Tanya's--or maybe it was Tori's or Tabitha's--hand. *You look exactly alike.*

"Hey, Casey." Jake strolled up and looked around. "Where's Sumo?"

Sumo jammed a paintbrush into a paint jar, got some red paint on the brush and took a step toward Casey.

"Uh, he's around."

Jake pointed to Hieronymus. "Who are you?"

Casey jumped in. "Um, you can't talk to him while he's working. You know how actors are. They've got to stay in character. Just call him Hieronymus."

Sumo raised a paw in greeting.

Jake shrugged. "Okay."

Casey made a face. "Sorry about missing the game."

Jake checked his cell phone for the time. "It doesn't start for two hours. Call Sumo and we can catch it later."

"Yeah, sounds good."

"Are a lot of people coming today?"

"Mom sent out the usual social media blasts, but it was last minute. She said a bunch of Brea Campers are coming."

A horn tooted. Casey and Sumo turned to see a big Brea Campers bus pull into the parking lot and park. Small faces and little hands were pressed against every window. Two more buses rolled in behind it.

"Holy, moly, joly," Sumo squeaked.

THIRTY

Sumo grabbed Casey's arm and dragged him away from Jake and the girls. "Your mom said a bunch of campers were coming—not the entire kid universe. We're never going to get out of here. I'm going to be a stupid hamster forever."

"Get a grip. I've got an idea how we can speed things up." Casey called over to Jake, Tanya, Tabitha, and Tori. "Grab those little tables and put them next to the long one."

The bifold doors of the first bus opened and a tall woman in tan shorts and a Brea Campers Counselor T-shirt got out. Behind her little people with short, sturdy legs jumped from the bus step to the ground and followed her. The counselor strode about twenty feet ahead of them, whipped around, brought a whistle to her lips, and shrilled out a blast guaranteed to break the sound barrier. The kids stopped so fast they ran into each other.

"Buddy up!" the counselor bellowed.

"Yes, Miss Jamie."

Casey steered Sumo back to the long table. "Here's the thing. We've got all these kids, a hundred posters and only a few jars of paint."

"Yeah, so?"

"We don't want to call Mom and ask for more paint because then we'll never get out of here."

"Are you getting an idea?"

Dylan scratched his ear with his back paw and whined. *Are you getting us into trouble?*

Casey opened a water bottle. "We'll add water to the jars of paint, so we'll have enough paint." He grinned. "Before you know it, we'll be watching the game."

Dylan's stomach gave a happy growl. *And eating junk food.*

"Sumo, take a stack of posters, spread them out on the table, and start painting HH on them as fast as you can."

"Your mom said to paint Hieronymus in the corner."

She did. Listen to him, Casey.

"Hieronymus is too long, and it will take too much paint."

Dylan flicked his left ear. *You know Mom will check.* Dylan watched Casey add water to the jars of paint and shake them. Water floated to the top and paint sank to the bottom. *Something doesn't look right.*

"Okay." Sumo waved two paws in the air and backed off. "I'm just a hamster."

You need to call Mom.

Casey signaled to Jake, Tanya, Tori and Tabitha. "Hurry up with those tables."

Sumo spread the posters out on his table, dipped his brush into a jar of red paint and got to work. "It's kind of runny."

"Mom said it was fast-drying poster paint. Don't worry about it."

Sumo stuck the brush into the paint jar, swished it around, and tried it again.

Dylan watched the paint from Sumo's brush drip onto the poster and run. *Not looking good.*

"What about us?" Tanya or Tabitha or Tori asked after the last table was brought over.

"Jake," Casey pointed, "take a bunch of posters and give some to the girls. Everybody spread them out on the tables. Get a paintbrush, a jar of paint, and start painting HH in the corner of each poster."

"Then what?" Jake reached for the stack of posters.

"When the kids come out of Brea's Ice Cream, pass a poster to Hieronymus to give to the kids."

"Sure," they said and got to work.

Miss Jamie waited until the other Brea Campers' buses were unloaded and two other counselors herded the kids across the parking lot. "All right, Brea Campers," she commanded and gave another ear-splitting blast, "follow me. No sudden moves!"

"How's it coming?" Casey waved a paintbrush toward Tanya, Tabitha, and Tori, and a red paint flew off his brush.

The girls nodded in unison.

Jake squinted up at the swaying palm trees. "The wind keeps blowing dirt and gunk onto the wet paint." He picked something off and tossed it away.

"I know," Tanya or Tori or Tabitha complained. "I've got twigs and dirt on mine."

"Keep painting. The kids only have a choice of chocolate or vanilla ice cream inside the ice cream shop." Casey painted HH on the corner of his poster. "Crystal will hustle them through in record time."

A puff of wind blew an ear across Dylan's face, and he shook his head. *I hope Crystal saves some vanilla ice cream for me.* Dylan watched Sumo slop HH in the corner of a poster. *I hope the kids can't read.*

"This is hard." Sumo held a poster down with a pink paw and painted with the other. "The wind keeps moving the posters around on the table."

"Yeah, but the wind will make the paint dry faster." Casey picked up the jar of paint and read the label. "Oh-oh. This says, 'Do not add water to the poster paint'."

Told you. Call Mom.

"Does it matter?"

Yeah. Call Mom.

"Nah."

Dylan shook his head, whined low, and put his muzzle on his paws. *You never listen to me.*

Sumo dipped his brush into the paint again. "I can't wait to get out of this dumb costume and go watch the game. I'm starving." He rubbed his stomach with a paw, leaving a smear of red paint behind.

Once again, Miss Jamie's beloved whistle blew. "March, Brea Campers!"

The kid troopers obeyed until they saw Hieronymus and Dylan.

"That's Hieronymus!" "Hieronymus books are my favorite." "Look! That's a dog!"

Dylan bolted upright in the basket and looked around. *Where?*

"Can we pet the dog?" "The dog is cute." "Why is his hair sticking straight up?" "I have a hamster named Hieronymus."

The kids broke rank, running toward Dylan and Hieronymus, their little legs pistoning.

There's so many of you. Dylan shrank back into the basket. *Casey! Help!*

"Race you there!" "Stop pushing!" "I'm telling!"

"Casey, do something." Sumo forgot about being quiet. "We're being attacked by the munchkin mob!"

The whistle sounded again. "Ice cream first, Brea Campers!"

"No!" came the kid chorus, ignoring her and crowding around Dylan and Hieronymus.

"Quit pushing!" "Am not!" "I'm telling!"

Casey, help! Small hands reached for Dylan, grabbing ears, paws, and his bandana. *Get your own bandana!*

"Leave the dog alone, Brea Campers!" Miss Jamie ordered.

"Okay!" "Hieronymus!"

Small people muscled their way past Miss Jamie and latched onto Sumo's legs, hugging his knees and together they started to rock.

"Hey, let go!" Sumo's front paws flew up and his little, pink back paws tried kicking himself free. He lost his balance and landed on his stubby tail. "Casey!"

Dylan tummy-crawled forward and peeked over the rim of the basket. Short people in shorts and short sleeved T-shirts filled the parking lot and were running his way. *We need Mom.*

Sumo rolled over onto his round stomach, buns up in the air, and rocked side-to-side, struggling to get to his paws. Campers happily petted him when he rocked their way.

"Hieronymus is soft!" "Why is his tail so short?"

Sumo struggled to his paws and shouted, "Back! Get back!"

"Girls," Jake stopped painting and waved his paintbrush in Hieronymus's direction, "is that Sumo?"

The girls stopped painting, raised six eyebrows at Jake, and shrugged. "Of course."

Casey worked himself between the kids and Dylan.

"Who wants an autographed poster of Dylan and Hieronymus?"

"Me!" "Me!" "I'm first!"

Miss Jamie brought the whistle up to her lips.

Casey reached for her arm. "I've got this."

Dylan's paws felt for his ears. *I haven't got any hearing left.*

Sumo poked a tiny paw in Casey's ribs and backed away. "Tell your mom I quit."

Casey snagged Sumo by his plaid vest and announced, "Kids meet Hieronymus."

"Yay!" "Yay!"

Casey dropped his voice to a whisper. "The sooner we get these posters handed out, the sooner we can watch the game."

"You owe me."

And me.

"Okay, kids." Casey and Sumo started handing out posters like they were dealing a deck of cards. "Girls, Jake," Casey called, "keep at it."

At the tables, Tabitha, Tanya, and Tori were painting HH on the posters like crazy.

The wind whirled around them and Jake raised his voice, "Casey, I'm out of paint. I'll help hand out posters."

"See," Casey said to Sumo, "nothing to worry about."

You always say that, Dylan whined, *and you're always wrong.* He scooted to the edge of the basket and hooked his paws over the edge to watch Casey, Sumo and Jake.

"Here's your poster," Casey said to each kid. He nudged Sumo. "Look at these happy faces."

Dylan settled back in the basket. *Maybe you're right.*

When the kids tipped the posters up for a look, the paint ran like a greyhound.

"Agh!" "Yeck!" "It's on my shirt!" "Miss Jamie!"

"Casey, do something." Sumo waved his front paws in the air. "Call your mom!"

A big gust of wind came out of nowhere. The posters from the tables became flying saucers of dripping paint.

Dylan ducked. A poster skimmed his topknot and red paint glopped onto his ear. *Grr!* His paw shot up and swiped at his ear, smearing the paint onto his muzzle. He sent his tongue out for a lick. *Awful.* Another poster zinged his way. He rolled to his side, smearing red paint onto the white material. *Yikes!* He pushed up with his paws and stepped in the paint. *Ick!* Scooting back, Dylan crouched low and stared at the red paw prints on the white material. *Are my paws really that big?*

Miss Jamie raised her whistle and got slammed full in the face with a flying poster. "Eek," she squeaked.

"Are you okay, Miss Jamie?" Casey ran toward her just as the poster slithered down her camp shirt, leaving a red streak on her tan shorts and tennis shoes. Miss Jamie staggered back. Her eyes went wild, and her hands went around her throat. "Ack!"

Dominick rushed out of Brea's Ice Cream and looked around. "What's going on?"

Oh-oh.

THIRTY-ONE

Casey kicked back in his chair and licked cherry vanilla ice cream off his spoon. "Today went okay."

Sumo's eyes popped. "Miss Jamie swallowed her whistle. Crystal had to call the paramedics to take her to emergency." He went back to his ice cream. "Did you see how Dominick jumped in and did that Heimlich maneuver thing? I thought that only happened on TV."

Dylan kicked his ice cream dish out of the way and used his paws to rumple up his towel. He flopped down and stretched out onto his side. *Maybe now Miss Jamie will stop blowing that dumb whistle.* He raised his head and sniffed. *Something smells good.* Snuffling the towel with his muzzle, he found a dribble of vanilla ice cream and licked it off. *Happy surprise.*

"Did you know," Tanya or Tori or Tabitha asked, "Dominick wants to be a doctor?"

"No kidding." Casey took another bite of ice cream. "Since when?"

She stared at him. "Since forever."

"Casey's right." Jake took the last bite of ice cream and

put his dish on the table. "Today was a fun day." He pointed at Sumo. "Why didn't you tell us you were Hieronymus?"

Sumo slanted his eyes at him. "Are you nuts? You would've told everybody."

"Are you nuts?" Jake shot back. "You get all the fun. Dressing up like Hieronymus would've been a blast." He wadded up his napkin and tossed it at Casey. "Next time your mom needs somebody, tell her to ask me."

Casey made a face. "Are you serious?"

Dylan blinked up at Jake. *You want to be a hamster?*

Jake wiped his mouth with the back of his hand. "Don't tell anybody but I want to be an actor."

"No way," Tanya, Tabitha and Tori chimed.

"Yeah, well," Jake tossed it off, "beats being an accountant like my dad. That'd be so boring to move numbers around all day."

"It's weird thinking about being something." Casey put his ice cream dish on the table and looked Dylan. "You know, like when you grow up."

Dylan sat up and nuzzled Casey's leg. *We're going to be dog trainers.*

"Not me." Sumo dug into his ice cream with his fingers and shoved a toffee piece into his mouth. "All I have to be is rich."

"You must dream of doing something, Sumo," Tanya or Tori or Tabitha insisted.

"Well, yeah." He wiped his hands on the front of his shirt. "I'm going to be a rich, famous baseball player."

Wow. Can I come to all your games, wear a team T-shirt, and eat junk food?

She pointed to her sisters. "We're going to be event planners and do big parties and weddings."

"Awesome, Tori," said Sumo. "You can do my mom's next wedding."

How did Sumo know she is Tori?

Tori smiled brightly. "Your mom would be good for business." She turned to Casey, "What about you?"

Dylan laid his muzzle on Casey's thigh. *Tell them.*

Casey pulled Dylan onto his lap and reached around him to pick up his dish of ice cream.

"Hmm." Casey held the ice cream dish in front of Dylan and made swirly patterns in the ice cream.

Dylan snuffled the side of Casey's face. *Are you going to eat that?*

"Mom wants me to go into business with her." Casey stuck his finger in the ice cream and gave Dylan a taste. "You know, publish books and stuff."

"Like that's going to happen," Sumo laughed. "You hate reading."

"Yeah." Casey put the dish on the table again and hugged Dylan close.

Dylan laid his head against Casey's chest. *Tell them about you and me.*

Sumo shoveled more ice cream into his mouth. "Casey's afraid to tell his mom he wants to be a dog trainer." He grinned and ice cream dribbled out. He caught it with the back of his hand.

Tanya, Tori, and Tabitha clapped their hands together. "Do it!"

Casey shook his head. "Mom's all into college. She'd have a fit if she knew I wanted to train dogs."

I'm a dog. Dylan raised his muzzle to Casey's face. *What's the matter with that? Whine.*

"Nah," Sumo argued, "your mom's cool."

Listen to Sumo.

"Yeah," Jake agreed.

"Forget it." Casey tossed his spoon into his dish. "Being a dog trainer is just a dumb dream."

"Hey, it's awesome, if it's what you want," Sumo argued and then mumbled, "unless you're scared to try."

Casey straightened Dylan's bandana. "Maybe I am."

Dreams should scare you, Dylan slurped the side of Casey's face, a*nd make you want to try harder.*

"Your mom would get it," Jake chimed in. "She started her business by herself. That had to be hard."

Dreams are hard. That's why most people just dream about them.

"Yeah."

"Go for it," Tabitha insisted. "Tanya, Tori and I dream about all kinds of stuff."

"That's different. You have each other."

We have each other.

Casey held onto Dylan and rocked back in his chair. "It costs a lot of money to open a dog training business. Where am I going to get that?"

"Easy," Sumo grinned. "I'll start a marketing company and do all your social media. With my help you can't lose. Once you're rich, your mom will forget you didn't go to college." He clapped his hands together and grinned again. "Problem solved."

"Wow." Casey dropped the chair down and shifted Dylan on his lap. "You'd give up being a rich, famous baseball player and do that for me?"

Sumo's grin went bigger, "I'm still going to be a rich, famous baseball player. Because of you, now I have to start a business so I can make you rich."

Thanks, Sumo. You're our best friend.

"That's sweet," Tanya or Tabitha or Tori said, "but how are you going to do that when you move to Paso Robles?"

Sumo lost the grin. "What do you mean, Tanya?"

She looked at her sisters but got no help. "Your mom was talking to our mom, and your mom said she's moving to Paso Robles after the wedding."

Oh, no.

"Never happen." Sumo waved a hand in the air and let it drop. "The estate's been in our family for almost a hundred years." He added a weak laugh. "Mom's walk-in closet is the size of a football field." He slid a look at Casey and Dylan. "She'd never move to Paso Robles."

Dylan squirmed against Casey. *Do something. Sumo is our best friend.*

"No way," Casey agreed and rubbed Dylan's ears, "but if that happens you can always live at our house. Right, Little Buddy?"

Arf!

"Hey, Casey," Jake nudged him, "here comes your mom."

"Quiet everybody," Casey whispered. "Don't say anything about the dog trainer thing."

"Hi, Ms. D," Tanya, Tabitha and Tori sang out.

"Hi, kids." She came over to Casey and glanced at the mess on the table. "Looks like I'm too late for ice cream."

"We finished with the posters early, Mom."

"Did you get some ice cream, too?" Mom leaned down to pet Dylan.

Only a bit. Dylan pawed the air. *Seconds?*

She started to run her hands through his fur but stopped. "Why does Dylan have red paint in his topknot and ear?"

"Red paint? Really, Little Buddy?" Casey turned Dylan

around, "Must have been when you were having so much fun helping Hieronymus paint."

Grr.

"Did a lot of people show up?"

Casey glanced around the table at the others before shaking his head. "Not really. Mostly the Brea Campers."

"That's a shame. So, there are a lot of posters left?"

"No." Casey jutted his chin toward the poster table. "All gone."

Her eyebrows drew together when she saw the clean table with the empty jars of paint and paintbrushes. "Casey, how did you get rid of a hundred posters?"

Casey hugged Dylan close to him. "It was a breeze. Right, Little Buddy?"

THIRTY-TWO

"Hold on." Casey nudged Dylan aside to open the front door.

Dylan wiggled between Casey's legs and stuck his face out. *Is it here?*

"Special delivery for Dylan Easter Donovan from Bernard Franco," a man in a navy suit said.

Yes! Dylan stepped closer.

"Thanks." Casey reached for Dylan's chain collar with one hand and with his other hand took the box tied with a huge peach ribbon from the messenger. After he shut the door Casey brought the box close to Dylan's muzzle. "I told you it would come today."

Let me see it.

"Now you can stop being a pest."

Dylan circled Casey's feet and looked up at him. *I'm the ringbearer not a pest.*

"We have to hurry," Casey started for the stairs, "or we'll be late for the wedding rehearsal."

Dylan charged up the stairs and ran into Casey's room.

He leaped onto Casey's bed and shook his buns in the air. *Arf! Open it up.*

"We'll look at it later." Casey tossed the box onto his bed. "I'm getting in the shower. Don't mess with anything."

Dylan parked his rump on the bed and slid his big brown eyes Casey's way. *Not me.*

As soon as Casey turned the shower on, Dylan snuffled the box. *Time to see my vest.*

The box slid across Casey's bed and Dylan slapped at it with his front paw. *What was with the ribbon?* Dylan teased the end of the ribbon away, letting the bow unravel. *Hooray!* He used his nails and dragged the ribbon aside. *Much better.*

Back to the box. Dylan tummy crawled forward and put both front legs on top of the box. He rocked side to side. The box caved in but didn't fall apart. Dylan put his buns in reverse and gnawed on a corner. *Ow!*

Dylan worked his mouth back and forth. *Something is stuck in my teeth. Agh! Agh!* He tried spitting it out. *There must be a better way.*

Dylan backed up and charged the box. He gave it one good swipe with his front paw and they both tumbled off the bed. The box landed in front of Dylan with a little bounce and the top flew off.

"Dylan, what's going on out there? Are you okay?"

Oh no. Casey's out of the shower.

"What are you doing?"

Nothing. Yet.

Dylan looked inside the box. *It's wrapped in tissue paper. Really?* Dylan latched onto the tissue paper with his front teeth, hauled back and shook his head. The peach silk vest sailed out and landed on the floor.

My first vest. Dylan's heart soared like a kite. *Just the way I remembered it.*

Casey came out of his bathroom wearing shorts and pulling a T-shirt over his head. "Dylan! You've been in the box."

Dylan turned away. *Prove it.*

Casey bent down and raised Dylan's muzzle up. "You've got cardboard stuck in your teeth." Casey used his index finger to flick the pieces out of Dylan's canines and incisors.

I just wanted to see.

"Bernard won't let you wear this if you get drooly marks on it." Casey held up the vest and checked it out. "Looks fine to me." He wadded the vest up and tossed it onto his chair. "Let's go." Casey started walking toward the door but stopped and pulled his cell phone out.

Dylan bumped into him. *Hey!*

"Sorry. I promised Mom I'd text her when we leave." He tapped the cell phone a few times with his thumbs. "Okay, now we're ready."

Outside Casey helped Dylan into the bike trailer. "When we get to Sumo's house, we need to find Bernard Franco." Casey waited while Dylan settled himself. "Did I tell you he's also the wedding coordinator? Sumo says Bernard's been ordering everyone around all day."

Bernard has a lot of rules. Dylan's shoulders slumped. *What if I mess up tomorrow?*

"I know you're a little worried about being the ringbearer." Casey got closer. "It's a big job but you'll be great. Some four-year old named Fiona is the flower girl, but she doesn't know zip."

Dylan flicked his ears. *You're no help.*

"Look, you don't need to know anything. Bernard will

tell everyone what to do." Casey grinned. "If you get it wrong, it doesn't matter. Ms. Modragon is always getting married. You'll get another chance."

Dylan looked up. *Will I get another vest?*

Casey zipped up the screen on Dylan's bike trailer, swung his leg over his bike and took off.

Dylan sighed and gave in to a quick snooze.

"We're parking in front," Casey said when they got to Sumo's house. He strapped his helmet to the handlebars and knelt to unzip the screen on Dylan's bike trailer. "Maybe Sumo can come over after the rehearsal. We can watch a movie or do something."

Dylan waited while Casey hooked his leash to his collar. *Does 'do something' mean food?*

Before Casey could ring the doorbell, Ingrid opened the door. Inside the house a man and a woman were shouting, each one competing for first place.

Casey waited. "Uh, hi, Ingrid."

"Hi, Casey and Dylan." She gave a thin smile and moved back to let them in.

Casey and Dylan stepped inside. "What's going on?"

"Ms. Modragon and Mr. Winters are in the piano room," she flinched when something crashed against the wall, "discussing the wedding."

"Where's Sumo?"

"He's in his room." She bent down and scratched Dylan's ear. "Are you ready for your big day?"

Crash!

"Be reasonable, Selena," an angry man's voice yelled.

"There's no way," a woman's really angry voice insisted. *Crash! Crash!*

"At least she can't throw the piano," Casey laughed. He hooked a thumb over his shoulder. "Can we go upstairs?"

"Yes. Please tell Sumo to hurry up. Mr. Franco is on the east lawn." Ingrid checked her watch. "The wedding rehearsal starts in fifteen minutes. The rest of the wedding party has already arrived."

Dylan perked up. *Are the dozen swans here?*

"Okay."

"Come into the kitchen after the rehearsal," Ingrid called after them. "I've made something special for you, Sumo and Dylan."

"Thanks, Ingrid."

Thanks, Ingrid.

Dylan trailed after Casey and up the winding staircase. *Something is wrong here. No one is happy.*

The door to Sumo's bedroom suite was open. "Sumo?" Casey and Dylan went inside and gave the big room the once-over. "This is weird. Ingrid said he was here."

They walked through the sitting room, past the pool table, the pinball machine and big screen TV.

Dylan scented the air and pulled Casey toward Sumo's bedroom. *This way.*

"Okay."

Sumo was wearing a starched white shirt, a tie and dress pants and was sitting cross-legged on the floor near his bed. He was tossing a baseball in the air and catching it in his glove. Sumo kept his eyes on the ball. "Hi."

"Hi." Casey sat on the floor next to Sumo's bed and stretched out his long legs. "Why are you wearing those dorky clothes?"

Sumo rolled a shoulder. "Mom said I had to look good today." He tossed the ball again but tipped his head toward his bed and the Angels T-shirt thrown across it. "Maybe we can play catch or something later."

"Yeah, sure."

Whine. Dylan's heart sighed. *You are one lonely kid.*

"Hi, Dylan." Sumo didn't look at him but tossed the ball again and caught it with his glove. "Thanks for doing the ringbearer thing," he gave a half laugh, "but I'm not sure wearing a peach vest is worth it."

Dylan thought about that. *Maybe not but you're worth it.*

Sumo went back to tossing the ball. Casey let go of Dylan's leash and Dylan drifted around Sumo's room sniffing, looking for anything interesting. *Nothing. How could this be a kid's room? Everything is so neat.* Dylan found the trashcan under Sumo's desk and stuck his face in. *Empty. No candy wrappers. No half-eaten bags of Cheetos or Doritos. No open cans of soda. Very disappointing.*

Casey leaned back against Sumo's bed. "What's up?"

Sumo let the ball drop and roll away. "We're moving to Paso Robles after the wedding."

No! Dylan whipped around, bolted over, and muscled his way in between Sumo and Casey. *Say it isn't so!*

Casey pulled Dylan close to him. "I heard your mom and Mr. Winters yelling in the piano room. What's that all about?"

Sumo tossed his glove aside. "Mom says Morgan's house is too small. She says it's only seven thousand square feet and she couldn't possibly live in a rabbit hutch. Mom wants Morgan to build a bigger house."

"His name is Michael."

"Whatever."

"Maybe you'll luck out," Casey tried a grin, "and she'll call off the wedding."

Sumo leaned forward, resting his arms on his knees. "Are you kidding? Weddings are her life."

Casey made a face. "She sounded pretty mad."

"Only about the house." Sumo leaned back. "She'll get her way. She always does."

Casey reached for Sumo's glove and pounded his fist into it. "What are you going to do?"

Dylan stretched out alongside Casey and put his muzzle across his lap. *What are we going to do? Sumo's our best friend.*

Sumo scrubbed his hands over his face. "I'm stuck. I have to go." He dropped his hands into his lap and avoided looking at Casey. "Here's the really sucky part. Ingrid can't go with me to Paso Robles. She has to stay here and run this house."

You'll be all alone. Dylan whined. *Poor kid.*

Casey moved Dylan aside and pushed to his feet. "Your mom can't just take you to Paso Robles." Casey reached for Dylan's leash. "All your friends are here."

You need to stay with us.

Sumo hugged his knees. "Her mind is made up."

"We'll think of something. But right now, we have to get downstairs. Everybody is here."

"Go on." Sumo stayed put. "I'll be down in a minute." He tried a smile. "They can't rehearse without me, right?"

"Right." Casey huffed out a breath and tugged on Dylan's leash. "C'mon, Little Buddy."

This wedding is not going to be fun.

When they reached the east lawn, Casey gave a low whistle. "The place looks great. Bernard has been really busy. Wow, there must be forty rows of white chairs out here." Casey lifted Dylan up so he could see the lake. "Ms. Modragon got her swans. I guess no wedding is complete without them."

Dylan craned his neck to check out the swans, then

turned back to Casey. *They're just a bunch of big white ducks. So what?*

"See the man standing under the white arbor?" Casey pointed to a tall man with a round, friendly face. "That's Reverend Monahan."

Reverend Monahan was holding a black book and smiling at no one in particular. "Ms. Modragon uses Reverend Monahan for all her weddings." Casey shifted Dylan and counted on his fingers. "This is her fourth wedding." He frowned and counted again. "Maybe fifth."

Reverend Monahan must be a very busy man.

Musicians sat off to the side, tuning instruments and waiting to play. Bernard Franco, wearing aviator sunglasses and holding a portable microphone, was directing traffic. "You, yes you." Bernard flapped a hand in the air toward a waiter. "I specifically said champagne flutes, not wine glasses."

The waiter mumbled something and scurried away with his tray.

Bernard caught sight of Casey and Dylan and spoke into the mic, "At last. You are here." He motioned them over and stood on tiptoe, looking beyond them. "Where is Sterling? We need to begin. Ms. Modragon is most precise about starting on time."

"Sumo's coming." Casey put Dylan on the ground and changed the subject. "Thanks for sending Dylan's vest today. He was very excited to get it. Right, Little Buddy?"

Arf!

Bernard clapped his hands together. "My pleasure, for the little doggie! I wrapped the vest in tissue paper myself so it would be perfect for the wedding. Silk wrinkles so easily."

Dylan pawed Casey's leg. *You wadded my vest up and throw it on your chair.*

"Not now, Little Buddy."

A small girl raced over and grabbed the hem of Bernard's jacket with both hands.

"Oh no, no, honey," Bernard pried her fingers away from the soft fabric, "this is silk." He turned her toward Casey and Dylan. "Meet Fiona. She is Ms. Modragon's flower girl."

"Ew!" Fiona screwed up her face and pointed at Dylan. "Is that a dog?"

Very good, I'm a dog.

"Now, now, Fiona." Bernard patted her shoulders. "Dylan is Ms. Modragon's ringbearer."

"I'm the flower girl and I'm more important than the ringbearer." Fiona stuck her tongue out at Dylan.

I'm the ringbearer and Ms. Modragon can't get married without me. Dylan cocked his head and let his tongue fall out of his mouth. *So there.*

Casey reached down and brushed Dylan's topknot out of his eyes. "Behave," he whispered.

Why? She started it.

"I don't like you." Fiona spun around on the heels of her white sandals and took off.

Good.

The wedding party drifted over. "Sit, everyone. Sterling will be here shortly and then we will begin." Bernard and his microphone ordered the waiters to serve champagne. Bernard nodded to the musicians, and they launched into their first song.

Everybody waited.

And waited.

Whine. Dylan blinked in the hot sun. *Where's Sumo?*

Casey brought his cell phone out and texted Sumo. He waited a minute and then tried calling. "That's strange. It went to voicemail. He's probably on his way over right now."

Or not.

Twenty minutes later in the hot sun, the musicians had played their songs, the champagne was disappearing, and the wedding party was getting restless.

Bernard hurried over to Casey and Dylan. "Ms. Modragon has been texting me every ten seconds. Where. Is. Sterling?" He held a fist up to his lips and swiveled his head, searching the crowd. "She won't come out of her room until Sterling gets here."

Dylan rubbed against Casey's leg. *She may be in her room forever.*

"We'll go get Sumo." Casey picked up Dylan's leash. "He probably just lost track of the time."

Dylan trotted alongside Casey. *I don't think so.*

Once they were out of sight, Casey and Dylan raced across the lawn and into the house. They took the stairs two at a time and jogged down the long hallway to Sumo's suite. "Sumo?"

Dylan didn't bother to scent the air but barreled into Sumo's bedroom. *Sumo?*

Casey skidded to a halt behind him. "Oh no, Little Buddy."

No Sumo.

THIRTY-THREE

"We're searching the area and Lieutenant Kellan has ordered the K-9 Unit in." Sergeant Yelin surveyed the grounds. "Ingrid, how big is the property?"

"Eleven acres." She gestured around her. "Besides the main house, there's a guest house, a boathouse, an indoor pool house, a six-car garage and the horse stables."

Sergeant Yelin nodded. "I talked with Ms. Modragon, but she wasn't much help. She says she's been busy planning her wedding and hasn't seen Sumo since last night." He let that sink in, choosing his next words carefully. "Was Sumo upset because his mother's getting married again?"

Yes! Dylan danced on all four paws. *Arf!*

Ingrid nodded and chose her words carefully. "Last night Ms. Modragon told Sumo they're moving to Paso Robles after the wedding."

Sergeant Yelin waited. "Was he upset enough to run away from home?"

"I don't know." Her lower lip trembled, and she turned to Casey. "Sumo is attached to his cell phone. Why would he turn it off?"

Because he doesn't want to be found.

Chatter came from Sergeant Yelin's radio, and he stepped away. When he came back, he jutted his chin toward the main house. "Lieutenant Kellan wants Casey and Dylan to join him in Sumo's room."

Ingrid put a hand over her heart. "Have they found something?"

"Casey and Dylan were the last ones to see Sumo. The Lieutenant is hoping they can tell him if anything is missing from Sumo's room."

"Okay. Let's go, Dylan."

Walking across the lawn, Casey pulled out his cell phone and called Jake. "Hi, it's me. I need your help. Dylan and I are at Sumo's house for the wedding rehearsal." Casey started walking faster. "Anyway, Sumo's missing. The police are looking for him." Casey listened a moment. "Yeah, I want you to get the word out. You know, do the social media thing. Give them a description of Sumo." Casey listened some more. "Uh-huh. Uh-huh. Get ahold of Tabitha, Tanya, and Tori. Tell them to go to Sumo's favorite places." Casey stopped and scrolled through his phone. "I'm sending you the contact info for Brunhilda from the Brea Country Club. Remember her?" Casey gave a half laugh. "Yeah, she's scary but she can organize Dylan's Dog Squad and get them looking for Sumo."

Hurry. Dylan pawed Casey's thigh. *We've got to find him.*

Casey said goodbye and reached down to rub Dylan's head. "Keep your paws crossed, Little Buddy. Sumo needs our help."

They hustled toward the house. Inside Dylan pulled on his leash and charged up the stairs. Casey followed, taking the stairs two at a time.

"Hi, Officer Gregorian. Uncle Rory called."

Officer Gregorian moved aside. "Go in."

"Casey, Dylan." Rory lifted his hand in a wave, broke away from his officers and came over.

Dylan tugged on his leash and Casey let it drop. Dylan took off, sniffing around Sumo's bed. *Sumo's ball and glove are gone.* He stood on his hind legs and worked his way down the bed. *No Angels T-shirt.* Dylan dropped down to all fours. *Arf!*

"What's Dylan doing?"

"Getting Sumo's scent."

"Good luck with that one. This room is cleaner than most hospital rooms. Poor kid. He's not even allowed to make a mess."

Dylan pawed at the shirt, tie, and dress pants on the floor. *Whine.*

"What do you know, Uncle Rory?"

"Not much. The property cameras show Sumo taking off on his bike, but it doesn't show in which direction."

Dylan glanced back at them. *Sumo should've been microchipped—like me.*

Casey held up his cell phone. "I talked to Jake. Sumo isn't with him. I told Jake to check with Tanya, Tabitha, and Tori. Brunhilda will organize Dylan's Dog Squad and search around Brea."

"That'll be a big help." He crossed his arms over his chest. "We've got a description out, but we don't know what Sumo is wearing. Any idea?"

Casey shrugged. "He lives in shorts and a T-shirt." Casey went over to Dylan and picked up Sumo's shirt from the floor. "He was wearing this earlier. We can use it to track him."

Rory considered this. "The K-9 Unit is on its way, but

they won't get here for a while. If you two can start tracking Sumo, that would be great."

Arf! Arf! Dylan angled his head up to Casey. *We need to get busy.*

"Dylan will try." Casey closed both hands into fists in front of him, then tapped his right fist on his left wrist. "Ready to go to work?"

Arf!

"Check in with me if you hear anything, okay?" Rory said.

"Yeah, sure." Casey picked up Dylan's leash and started out. "You'll be the first to know."

Casey waited until they reached the staircase to pull his cell phone out of his shorts pocket. He checked the screen. "Nothing from Sumo." He shoved his cell phone back into his pocket and led Dylan down the stairs. "I know what you're thinking. You're thinking I should've told Uncle Rory that Sumo is wearing his Angels T-shirt and his glove and baseball are gone."

I'm thinking you didn't tell Uncle Rory the truth.

"Sumo is our friend. It's not right for his mom to make him move to Paso Robles."

We need to do the right thing.

Casey clomped over to his bike, yanked his helmet off the handlebars and rested it on his hip. "I feel kind of bad asking everybody to look for Sumo. I'm just trying to buy some time until we can find him." Casey shook his head, tossed his helmet on the ground, and squared off in front of Dylan. "Look, just because we *think* we know where Sumo is doesn't mean we *really* know where he is."

Dylan dropped down to his stomach and rolled his big brown eyes up at Casey. *We both know where Sumo went.*

Casey plopped down on the grass next to Dylan.

"When we find Sumo, I'll have to call Uncle Rory. That stinks." He plucked at a blade of grass and tossed it aside. "Sumo left because he had no choice."

Sumo had a choice. He just didn't like what it was. Dylan flicked his ears and looked away.

"Don't get like that." Casey turned Dylan around, so he was facing him. "You know it's not nice to judge."

Dylan studied Casey. *It's not nice to make excuses.*

Casey stroked Dylan's ears. "What should we do, Little Buddy?"

Dylan whined at Casey. *You know what we should do.*

Casey heaved to his feet. "Yeah, you're right. Let's go find Sumo."

Arf!

Casey unzipped the front of Dylan's bike trailer and Dylan hopped in. *Ready to roll!*

THIRTY-FOUR

Casey parked his bike at the top of his driveway and took his helmet off. He strapped it to the handlebars and unzipped the front of Dylan's bike trailer. "Dylan, find Sumo."

Arf! Dylan didn't bother to scent the air. He shot across the driveway and down the sidewalk to their house. Sumo was sitting on their front doorstep, tossing a baseball, and catching it with his glove. Dylan planted his front paws on Sumo's knees and covered his face with canine kisses.

"Hey, Dylan, cut it out." Sumo laughed, elbowed Dylan aside and wiped the dog slobber off his face with the hem of his Angels T-shirt. "It hasn't been that long."

I'm a dog. Arf! It's been dog years.

Sumo tossed Casey the baseball. "How did you know I'd be at your house?"

Dylan pawed Sumo's arm. *I knew this one.*

Casey caught the ball on the fly. "Easy. We talked about playing catch. Your glove and baseball were gone. You left your dorky clothes on the floor."

Sumo ran a hand down the front of his Angels T-shirt. "Man, I'm never wearing a tie again."

Casey sat on the other side of Dylan. "We don't have much time. I promised Uncle Rory, I'd tell him if we found you."

Sumo squinted into the sun. "I shouldn't have taken off, but I just couldn't stick around. I had to do something."

"What are you going to do now?"

Stay with us.

"I don't know." Sumo's cell phone vibrated. He checked the screen. "It's a text from Ingrid."

"Ingrid's worried about you."

"She's the only one."

"Your mom was worried. She called the police."

Grr. She was not. Ingrid called the police. Sumo's mom didn't even come out of her room.

"If Mom hadn't needed me for the wedding rehearsal, she wouldn't have known I was gone."

"That's not true," Casey said lamely.

Yes, it is.

"You don't get it." Sumo's voice dropped. "My mom isn't like your mom. Your mom's on your case all the time. She cares." He read Ingrid's text, smirked, and put the cell phone in his pocket.

"What is it?"

Sumo wrapped his arms around his knees but turned his face to Casey. "We're not moving to Paso Robles tomorrow."

"No kidding. Your mom called off the wedding?"

Sumo's eyes popped. "Are you insane? No way. She's just postponing the move to Paso Robles until Marcus builds her a big house. Told you she'd get her way."

"His name is Michael."

"Whatever."

"Great." Casey grinned and rubbed his hands together. "That gives us enough time."

"For what?"

"To start our business."

"Start a business?" Sumo scowled. "What business?"

"You said you would help me with my dog training business someday but," Casey dragged this part out, "I'm thinking we could start a Lost and Found business right now."

"I don't get it."

Dylan wiggled happily between them. *I do.*

Casey shifted on the doorstep. "Dylan's got a great nose. He found Lily, Luca—you."

It was nothing. Besides, Sumo's always at our house.

"People could hire us to find their lost pets or missing persons. What do you say?"

Hurry up and say yes. Dylan swung his head from Casey to Sumo. *Then we'll always be together.*

"Forget it. You're dreaming." Sumo frowned. "We can't start a business. We're kids."

We can. Dylan gave Casey and Sumo a forty-two teeth grin. *You've got me and I've got a great nose.*

"So what if we're kids? I know we can do this."

"We're just kids," Sumo repeated. "Who would hire us?"

"I. Would." Casey pointed to his chest.

"You're just saying that."

"No way." Casey shot his hands in the air. "Look, if I don't believe in myself, why should anyone else?" Red washed over his face, and he added, "Kids can dream."

Dogs can, too.

"Sure, it sounds great, but I can't do this." Sumo made a

face. "I'm moving to Paso Robles after Mom gets her new house, remember?"

Maybe not. Dylan stretched his muzzle across Sumo's leg and stared up at him. *C'mon, Sumo. Think hard.*

"Wait," Sumo said slowly, and his face turned happy. Leaning back on his hands, he crossed his ankles, and wiggled his feet. "By the time the new house is built, Mom and Malcolm will be getting divorced."

Michael! His name is Michael.

"Michael."

"Whatever."

"Let's get started." Casey punched Sumo on the arm. "Dreams don't work unless you do."

Sumo raised his eyebrows. "Who said that?"

"John C. Maxwell."

Sumo snickered. "You know you're a lot like your mom."

"That's not so bad." Casey shrugged. "The three of us can do this. What do you say?"

I say yes.

"There's never been a Modragon who's worked for a living." Sumo grinned wickedly. "My mom will have a heart attack."

"We need a name for our business. You know, something that tells people who we are. What we do."

Dylan's Dog Squad.

"Right. Something catchy."

We already have something catchy. Dylan got to his paws. *Dylan's Dog Squad.*

Sumo thought hard. "How about Pet Detectives?"

"Nah. We can find more than pets."

"Casey, Dylan and Sumo—At Your Service?"

Get serious. Dylan's Dog Squad.

"That sounds like a limousine company, Sumo."

Right. What's a limousine?

Sumo chewed on his lower lip. "Your mom's a genius at this marketing stuff. Maybe we could ask her to help us?"

Casey shook his head. "This is our business. We need to do everything ourselves."

Casey! Sumo! Dylan dropped down, rolled over onto his back and waved his paws in the air. *Look at me. Hint, hint.*

Casey scratched Dylan under his muzzle. "Dylan will be doing most of the work. How about something simple, like Casey, Dylan and Sumo's Company?"

"Boring."

Dylan sighed and let his paws drop to his chest. *No joke.*

"Hey," Sumo sat up straight. "Why not Dylan's Dog Squad?"

About time. Dylan sighed again, rolled over onto his stomach and shook out his ears. *When we're in business, you'd better find people and pets quicker than this.*

"Perfect. We already have Dylan's Dog Squad volunteers." Casey held his hand palm up to Sumo. "Partners?"

"Partners." Sumo slapped his hand on top.

Arf! Arf! Dylan jumped up and put both paws on Casey's and Sumo's hands and wiggled his butt. *Partners!*

"We're officially in business."

"What do we need to do first?"

"First up, Dylan needs to pass the American Kennel Club Canine Good Citizen test."

Sumo nodded. "That will be great for advertising." He pulled out his cell phone. "I'll start working on the social media." He thought out loud, "We need a website. I can do that." He went back to work on his cell phone. "I'm getting some ideas."

"Just think, Little Buddy," Casey hugged Dylan close, "when you're AKC certified, you'll have your own vest. No more just dreaming about it." He smiled down at him. "All you've ever wanted."

I want what you want. Dylan leaned against Casey. *That's my dream.* Dylan raised his muzzle and snuffled Casey's cheek. *It always was.*

The End

DYLAN RETURNS IN DYLAN'S VILLAIN

CHAPTER 1

"Are you sure you weren't followed?"

Casey and Sumo exchanged looks and shook their heads.

You're our first client. Dylan gave a happy tongue-hanging-out-of-his-mouth grin to the small girl sitting cross-legged on the floor of the tree house. *Dylan's Dog Squad is officially in business!*

Holly hunched forward, put her elbows on her knees and whispered, "Let's get one thing straight. Everything we say is confidential. You know, like between a lawyer and a client."

Casey squirmed. "Are you in trouble?"

Holly's dark eyes darted left and right. "If you don't find Bailey, I'm dead." Her eyes bugged out and she slashed her right index finger across her throat.

"Whoa." Sumo's thumbs paused midair above his iPad. "When you called, you said Bailey was gone. You didn't say anything about dead."

"Stay on track," Holly ordered. "He's gone and I'm going to be dead if you don't get him back."

Yikes. Dylan wiggled his buns and nudged Casey. *This is a big case. Good thing we're on the job!*

"So, are we straight here? Everything is confidential?" Holly glanced over her shoulder before dropping her voice an octave. "If it's not, I'm outta here."

Dylan pawed Casey's leg. *We're sitting in Holly's tree house. Where would she go?*

"You bet. Everything is confidential," Sumo agreed. "We'll need some information from you." His fingers returned to his iPad, ready to go to work.

Casey cleared his throat. "How long has Bailey been missing?"

Holly squeezed her eyes shut, gave a small shake of her head, and counted fast to ten. When she opened her eyes, she zeroed in on them. "Bailey's been *gone* since breakfast."

Casey checked his cell phone for the time. "That's not very long to be missing."

Holly tossed her hands into the air. "Bailey is *gone*, not *missing.*"

"I don't get it," Sumo said. "What's the difference?"

Holly slapped both palms onto her knees. "Is English a second language for you? Bailey is *gone.* That means he's not *here.*" She paused. "He always comes back. Eventually." She hitched a shoulder and let it fall. "Sometimes he's gone for days." She pointed her finger at them. "Your job is to get him back now."

"All right." Casey moved on. "How old is he?"

Holly sat up straight. "Ten, like me."

"Okay. What color is his hair?"

"Black, like mine." Each hand grabbed a fistful of hair and pulled it away from her face. "Kind of spiky."

"Eyes?"

Her thumbs and index fingers formed two circles around her eyes. "Black, like mine."

Sumo looked up from his iPad. "How tall is he?"

She fluttered a hand over her head. "Same size as me."

Are you twins?

"Got it." Sumo nodded and thumb-tapped the info into the iPad. "What was Bailey wearing?"

She chewed on her lower lip. "A red and blue cape."

"That's it?" Casey frowned.

Holly tipped her head, thought, and nodded once. "Yeah."

Bailey must be very cold.

"Uh," Casey looked to Sumo but got no help, "do you have a picture?"

"Sure." Holly pulled a cell phone out of her back pocket, scrolled through her pictures, and worked the screen. "I just sent it to you."

Sumo's cell phone pinged, and Casey, Sumo and Dylan leaned together to look at the screen.

Dylan studied Bailey's picture—short spiky black hair, big ears, pale round-moon face, black beady eyes, big lips, big feet, long arms, and a yellow toothy grin.

"Whoa," Casey said. "Bailey is."

A really ugly kid.

"A chimp," Sumo blurted out.

"A kleptomaniac," Holly corrected.

Dylan looked up at Casey. *Huh?*

"Steals things," Casey explained.

Dylan took in the tree house crammed with stuff. A striped hammock, strung from corner-to-corner, was heaped with stuffed animal toys. A guitar was propped in the corner next to a tennis racket and boogie board. Backpacks were everywhere. Flip-flops, straw hats, and sweatshirts were piled next to a tricycle and bike helmet. Stacks of Amazon deliveries and mail lined the walls, blocking out the sun from the windows. *Bailey is one sticky-fingered chimp.*

"Look, I'm staying with my grandfather while Rachel, that's my mom, is on tour with her latest book."

Casey interrupted, "Why do you call your mom Rachel?"

Holly narrowed her eyes. "Do I really have to explain every little thing to you?"

It would help.

"Anyway, the San Diego Zoo has this big ribbon cutting ceremony thing coming up and Rachel is coming home on Wednesday. I'm supposed to be watching Bailey. So far, she and my grandfather don't know Bailey is gone." She sucked in a ragged breath. "I want to keep it that way. If they find out," the finger slashed across her throat again.

"You're dead," Casey finished.

"Hey!" Sumo waved both hands in the air. "I've got it! Your mom, your mom," he stammered, "is Rachel Langdon. Wow!" Sumo turned to Casey. "Remember when she spoke to our class last year? Hey, she never mentioned she had a daughter."

Holly gritted her teeth and muttered, "Never does."

"Wow, your mom is famous." Casey thought hard. "She's called something weird. Primo? Prima?"

"Primatologist," Holly and Sumo said together.

"Yeah." Casey elbowed Sumo. "You kept asking her all those dumb questions."

"They weren't dumb." Sumo elbowed him back. "Chimpanzees are so cool. They can see colors and details. They can run up to like twenty-five miles an hour and they're four times stronger than humans their size."

I can run faster than Casey.

Sumo went back to Holly. "Man, you're so lucky. You get to live up here with Bailey."

Holly blinked once. "Only Bailey lives in the tree house."

"Really?"

She scowled. "You think *I* live here?"

Sumo's cheeks burned. "Uh," he mumbled, "I mean it'd be so cool to have a chimp."

"Are you nuts?" Her black eyes flashed. "I'm a *servant* to that chimp. I've gotta eat my meals with him. Watch TV with him—*Animal Planet*. Like how many times can I watch that? I gotta take him for walks. Do you know what it's like to walk down the street with a chimp? Every time Rachel writes a new book, I gotta go on talk shows with him." She shuddered. "Rachel even makes me answer his fan mail." She tossed her hands into the air. "You wouldn't believe the dumb questions people ask."

Dylan, Casey, and Sumo kept quiet.

"Stuff like Does Bailey like Chunky Monkey Ice Cream? Who's Bailey's best friend? Does Bailey play on monkey bars? Does Bailey snore? What's Bailey's favorite color?" She narrowed her eyes. "My all-time favorite is when people ask if Bailey's my brother. Grr!"

Dylan flinched and wiggled closer to Casey. *She's kind of scary.*

"You're kidding!" Casey smirked. "People really ask that?"

You do look alike, same hair, same eyes. Dylan whined. *Same teeth.*

"Oh yeah, it's a riot having the other kids make fun of me. Calling me banana breath." She leaned closer. "When we were little, Rachel used to think it was fun to dress us alike."

Casey, Sumo, and I have matching Angels T-shirts.

"Your mom travels all over the world. It's pretty cool," Casey shrugged, "and you get to go, too."

"With a *chimp*?" She started tearing at the cuticle on her right index finger. "You don't know what it's like to have a famous mom. Everyone expects me to become a primatologist—just like her. *She* expects me to become a primatologist—just like her."

"We get it." Sumo pointed at Casey. "His mom was the same way. She has a children's book company and represents authors and illustrators. She was always telling Casey he had to go to college and then into business with her."

Dylan sighed. *Casey hates reading.*

"I finally got the guts to tell her I didn't want to." Casey pulled Dylan close. "Right, Little Buddy?"

Dylan put his muzzle on Casey's lap and licked his knee. *Right!*

Casey turned Dylan's bandana around and showed Holly the Dylan's Dog Squad logo. "So, Sumo, Dylan, and I started Dylan's Dog Squad. Dylan's going to take his American Kennel Club Canine Good Citizen test this week and he'll be certified."

Dylan pulled himself into a sitting position and puffed his chest out with pride. *I'll have my own vest with an AKC Canine Good Citizen patch.* Then Dylan's shoulders sagged. *Last time I didn't pass. I've got to pass. I can't let Casey down. He's counting on me.*

"Later," Casey stroked Dylan's ears, "we're going to have a dog training business. Do Search and Rescue. At first, I was scared to tell my mom but now she gets it."

"I told you she would," Sumo said. "Your mom's cool."

Casey, Dylan, and Sumo smiled.

"How nice for *you*." Holly stabbed the air between them with her bloody finger. "Where were we? Oh yeah, I'm supposed to be watching Bailey. Now he's gone and I'm going to be dead." She sat back. "Can you do the job or not?"

Arf!

Sumo waved his iPad. "Absolutely. Just a few more questions."

Casey started again. "How did Bailey, uh, become gone?"

Holly shrugged. "I guess I accidentally, sort of maybe, forgot to shut the tree house door this morning and he got out." She shrugged again. "When he gets out, he likes to," her voice trailed off, "collect things."

Dylan looked around. *The tree house is jammed full of stuff. You must forget a lot.*

Sumo considered this. "It's not like chimps run around Brea every day. Is he microchipped? Does he have a collar?"

"Just a collar. No chip."

No chip for the chimp.

"Great," Sumo said. "You could wait until someone finds him and then pick him up."

Arf! Pipe down, Sumo. This is our first case!

"You don't know much, do you? Only dogs and cats are domestic animals—not chimpanzees. Doesn't matter Bailey is famous. Doesn't matter Rachel is famous. If Animal Control gets ahold of Bailey, they'll toss him into the slammer."

Dylan pawed Casey's knee. *Slammer?*

Casey leaned down. "Jail."

"That might not be so bad," Sumo said slowly. "At least you'd get him back."

Holly's voice shot up. "Are you crazy or just dumb? How'd that look if Bailey gets arrested? My grandfather is Frank Matias—*Mayor* Matias."

Casey lifted his eyebrows. "You never said your grandfather is Mayor Matias."

Holly glared at him. "Well, I'm saying it now."

Oh-oh. Mom is friends with Mayor Matias.

"Well," Casey said lamely, "Bailey's been lucky so far. No one has seen him. Maybe he'll just come home."

"Yeah, well, Bailey has to get back quick. Like I said, the San Diego Zoo is having a big ribbon cutting ceremony. Rachel has this whole thing set up for the press. It's a really big deal," she huffed out a breath, "and Bailey—not me--gets to do the ribbon cutting."

You really don't like Bailey.

"Hey, that sounds fun." Sumo turned to Casey. "We should go."

Holly ignored Sumo and fisted a hand on her hip. "It's kind of hard to have a ribbon cutting ceremony with Bailey if there's no Bailey. We're running out of time."

Dylan whined. *Holly is making some excellent points.*

Casey nodded. "Have you thought of calling the police? My Uncle Rory is a Detective Lieutenant with Brea PD. I could ask him to put out a Be On the Look Out."

"Do I have to spell this out for you?" Holly swept a hand around the tree house. "Bailey has been on a crime spree, ripping off the neighbors." She clapped her hands together happily and leaned closer, "Lucky for me, no one will ever know. I've got a plan to get rid of all this."

"That's great," Casey nodded. "What's your plan?"

She smiled for the first time. "I'm donating it all to the Goodwill Society. There's a store by Stater Brothers on Imperial Highway."

Uh-oh. That's not a very nice plan.

Casey shifted his buns on the hard floor. "I'm pretty sure that's illegal."

Uh, yeah.

"So what? I'm desperate."

"You don't want to do that." Sumo looked up from his iPad and showed them the screen. "Google says messing with the US mail is a federal offense. You and Bailey would both end up in jail."

Just then a padded envelope slid off a tall stack of mail and thumped to the floor. Dylan pawed at Casey's leg. *It's too late for Holly to worry about jail. Bailey has already messed with the mail.*

"Bummer." Holly frowned. "I'll have to think of something else." She reached into the pocket of her shorts and put a fistful of twenties on the floor between them. "So how about it, Dylan's Dog Squad? Are you going to help me? Otherwise, I'm," she frowned.

"Dead," Casey and Sumo said together.

Whine.

ACKNOWLEDGEMENTS FOR DYLAN'S DREAM

Dylan—you're the best pup on or off planet. No pup compares to you.

Many thanks to Gina Capaldi, award winning illustrator, author, and friend. She graciously agreed to design the book covers for *Dylan's Dilemma* and for *Dylan's Dream*.

Many thanks to my incredibly talented writers and illustrators' group: Teri Vitters, Priscilla Burris, and Gina Capaldi. Their work leaves me speechless.

Many thanks to Marjorie McCowan, my awesome friend and writer, who always asked me to read one more chapter to her.

Many thanks to Detective Lieutenant Kelly Carpenter, Brea Police Department, for patiently answering my questions about police procedure.

Many thanks to Deborah Halverson and her invaluable editing comments.

Many thanks to Jonathan and Jynafer Yanez, the best consultants I could ever hope for.

I couldn't have done this without you.

SIMPLE SIGNS/HAND COMMANDS

- Applause/Yay/Hurrah: Hold your hands in the air and twist them a couple of times.
- Come: Extend both hands with index fingers pointing forward and up. Then bend your arms at the elbow, pull your fingers in toward your body.
- (Directions) Left: Raise hand and show thumb and index finger only. Motion to the left.
- (Directions) Right: Raise hand, show index and third fingers only. Cross index and third fingers. Motion to the right.
- Down: Point your index finger down and move your hand in a downward direction.
- Hi: Open hand to forehead and quickly move away in a salute.
- Hippo: Extend your index finger and little finger on both hands, and open and close them, having both hands meet in the middle—like a hippo's mouth.

- I Love You: Show your little finger, then your index finger and then your thumb.
- Jump: Make one hand flat. With your other hand, extend your middle and index fingers to make a 'little man' and have him jump up and down on your flat hand.
- Quiet: Bring your index finger to your lips.
- Sit Down: Have one hand flat/palm up. Take your other hand with index and middle fingers extended together in a slight hook to make the person's legs, and then sit them on your open palm.
- Stay: Use your thumb and little finger in a palm-down 'Y' shape. The movement is a forward thrust, not a downward slap. You are shoving the knuckles forward and a bit down.
- Stop: Extend your left hand, palm upward. Bring your right hand down to your left hand at a right angle.
- Watch: Use your index and third fingers. Thrust them forward.
- Work: Close both hands into fists in front of you, then tap your right fist on top of your left fist a couple of times in the wrist area.

ABOUT DYLAN EASTER TROY

Dylan was born on Easter in Daejeon, South Korea. His first owner bought him from Walmart.

At that time, I suggested basic dog training, but his first owner didn't think training was important. Dylan immediately destroyed his owner's apartment by chewing his way through electrical coverings, baseboards, and furniture. When Dylan ate the interior of his owner's BMW, his owner decided having a dog was too much work and didn't want him anymore.

I said I would take him.

Dylan spent twenty-seven hours in cargo hold to get to California. When I picked him up at Korean Air Cargo, Los Angeles International Airport, he was eighteen-months old, didn't know his own name, nor was he housebroken. We immediately started training and Dylan thrived. He loved agility training and competing with other dogs. His first big step came when he became certified as a Therapy Dog. Dylan enjoyed this but when he became American Kennel Club Canine Good Citizen certified, he went into service dog training, and became a Hospice Service Dog for people actively dying.

Additionally, Dylan's accomplishments include:

- Bilingual understanding: English and Korean
- Five hundred word and phrase vocabulary
- Basic American Sign Language and hand commands
- Ability to contact 9-1-1 with a special device
- Count to ten
- Television appearances
- Recognized in a feature article in the *Orange County Register* for his accomplishments
- Recognized by Baskin-Robbins for his accomplishments and his love of their vanilla ice cream
- Mascot for Cypress College in Cypress, CA.

Dylan is proof that there are no bad dogs. In fact, he's the smartest, best dog I've ever had or ever trained. Dogs need love, guidance, companionship, and a sense of purpose. At the end of Dylan's workday, he receives a bit of Baskin-Robbins vanilla ice cream.

He deserves it.

ABOUT THE AUTHOR

KATHLEEN TROY, JD; PHD

Kathleen Troy is a published author, children's book publisher, movie producer, writing and law professor at Cypress College, and former Director of Education and Development for the Archdiocese of Los Angeles. Kathleen is an active member of Sisters in Crime and Society of Children's Book Writers and Illustrators and has won several awards for middle grade and young adult books. Dog training is Kathleen's passion, and she has achieved recognition, most notably for training service dogs for hospice work.

Kathleen welcomes hearing from you. Please get in touch with her at www.kathleentroy.com.

STAY INFORMED

I'd love to stay in touch! You can email me at kathleen@kathleentroy.com

For updates about new releases, as well as exclusive promotions, visit my website and sign up for the VIP mailing list. Head there now to receive a free story

www.kathleentroy.com

Enjoying the series? Help others discover *Dylan's Dilemma* by sharing with a friend.

Made in the USA
Monee, IL
28 June 2023